AUTHORS NOTE

'The Tarot Kings world' is based in a magical future, but Venice is still the same as it has been for centuries. If you find yourself wondering where a location in the story is, any search on a modern map will be able to tell you where the action is taking place.

I have also included a guide to the world in the following pages should you want to use it as a reference at any point.

KING OF WANDS

THE TAROT KINGS
BOOK TWO

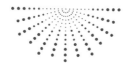

AMY KUIVALAINEN

THE NEW SERENE REPUBLIC

The New Serene Republic

The New Serene Republic of Venice is governed by a Council of Ten, made up of two representatives from each of the four ruling Houses, in addition to the Doge, who is always human, and his Grand Sorcerer. The current Doge is Giordano Loredan, and the Grand Sorcerer is Arkon Ziani.

The Ruling Houses of the Republic

House of Swords

The House of Swords, a.k.a. The House of Air, belongs to the air shifters and is predominately ruled by shedu. The shedu are capable of a human form and that of a winged lion. They originated from Babylon and ruled Constantinople before establishing themselves in Venice in 1562.

With their great wealth and knowledge, they have always helped govern and shape Venice from the shadows. At the dawn of the New Republic, in the year 2103 AD, the shedu were the first shifters to come into the light and take their rightful place on the Council of Ten.

The most prominent family and House of Swords representatives on the Council are the 'Golden-Winged Ones,' Carmella Aladoro and her son, Domenico. The sestieri of San Marco and San Paulo, despite being home to the richest humans in Venice, are shedu and other winged shifter territories.

House of Wands

The House of Wands, a.k.a. The House of Fire, belongs to the Djinn, other creatures of flame, and those who use fire-based magic. Djinn have a pure form that is rarely seen by outsiders, but they can take on a human's appearance when it serves their purpose.

The House of Wands is ruled over by the Djinn King, Zahir Matani, who represents them on the Council of Ten along with his second in command, Ashirah.

Along with the Djinn, the sestieri of Cannaregio and Santa Croce is home to human bankers, money lenders, and any other human or shifter with a fire affinity.

The only part of Cannaregio not ruled by the Djinn King, is the Jewish Quarter that falls under the jurisdiction of the Doge and the Council of Ten.

The Court of Wands monitors their domain by royal boat, which for fire beings proves not only the King's strength but also his authority, and rattling the mettle of those who wish to gain his favor.

The Djinn King is known for dispensing advice, justice, money, and deals to those who dare to consult with him.

House of Cups

The House of Cups, a.k.a. The House of Water, belongs to the sea serpent clans, other water shifters, and humans whose trade relies on the ocean, such as sailors, naval merchants, and fishermen.

They are governed by General Josefina Serpente D'Argento

and her nephew Nicolo, who represent the House of Cups and the Venetian Navy on the Council of Ten.

The sestieri of Castello is their domain along with the islands of San Giorgio Maggiore, Murano, Burano, and Torcello.

The House of Cups is responsible for the policing of all maritime activities and the shipbuilding yards.

Of all the Houses, they are the most militant, running the protection of the New Republic and policing the shipping lines between Venice and New Constantinople.

House of Coins

The House of Coins, a.k.a the House of Earth, is the only House dominated by humans and also accounts for all other types of magic-users, such as sorcerers, artificers, and alchemists. The sestieri of Dorsoduro and the Giudecca is home to scholars, writers, doctors, and scientists.

Their two representatives on the Council of Ten are Lorenzo Tera, an earth mage, and Frederico Romaro, a non-magical lawyer. When the House can't get what they need from their Council members, they often petition the Republic's Grand Sorcerer, who is answerable only to the Doge.

The Grand Duchy of Varangia - Enemies of the Republic

The Varangian Kingdom covers the areas of Eastern Europe from Russia to Romania, but also Hungary, Slovakia, and Poland. Their tsar, Arkadi Vasin, rules from the capital of Volgograd.

The Republic and Varangia have been at war for five years since the Varangians tried to take New Constantinople from the Turkish Empire. Trade partners to the Republic, New Constantinople sought aid from the Venetian Fleet and managed to defeat the Varangians, pushing them back to Romania.

Afterward, the Varangians declared the Republic as enemies and have since been working to take Croatia from Venice's rule.

Varangians abhor magic and magical creatures, encouraging the eradication of all non-humans within and outside the borders of their empire.

The Tsar has only one magical advisor: the famed Wolf Mage, rumored to be of Saint Olga of Kyiv's bloodline. The Wolf Mage wields the saint's power against the Republic's Grand Sorcerer and the Republic's army.

THE LAST ANCIENT WONDER

*T*here were many stories about Zahir the Eternal. Over time, they had grown more outlandish, exaggerated, terrifying, and magical, much like those about the King of the Djinn himself.

When asked which stories were true, Zahir had always replied, with a wink and a smile, that they all were.

If you tried to point out the tales that couldn't possibly be real for some reason or another, you would be invited to prove him wrong.

No one ever could.

One story about Zahir went as follows...

The year was 492 BC, and the events took place in the city of Babylon. The powerful Djinn King had been enslaved to the Persian throne. He had been used many times for his power of foresight and prophecy, so the great king Darius demanded that Zahir look into the future to the land of the Greeks, where Darius planned to make his next conquest.

Zahir asked for three days and nights to summon his most powerful visions. This, the great Darius granted.

On the dawn of the fourth day, Zahir once again was summoned before the throne.

"Oh, wise and divine king of kings, I have spent all of my power to divine the answers you seek," Zahir declared. "The great Persian king will burn Athens to the ground." This prophecy was met with much cheering by the courtiers...until Zahir held up his hand.

"But—" he continued, "I have also seen that Persia will need more than the strength of your army in order to accomplish this glorious victory. I must travel with you to the land of the Greeks and appear before their Senate as a freeman, like themselves, to spread fear and ensure they bow to you."

"And if I refuse?" Darius demanded, for freeing a djinn as powerful as Zahir was a high price to pay.

"If you refuse, you will die defeated by these backward tribes, which are too ignorant to give you the respect you deserve. As a broken man, your body will be covered in wax, and the great glory that you should be eternally remembered for will pass to another empire."

Darius refused to give his ruling on the matter until the day their fleet sailed into the Cyclades' blue waters. Finally, he summoned Zahir.

"You have served my family and this throne faithfully for a hundred years. I know what you want of me, but I am still reluctant to give it and miss your wise council in the future."

Zahir bowed low, ever the faithful servant. "Great king, I have served your throne so well, and you most of all, because of my deep love and devotion to Persia. Free me, and I will serve you still. You need no ring binding me to you for that," Zahir assured him.

Pleased by that announcement, Darius took the dull bronze ring engraved with sigils from his finger and passed it to Zahir, granting him his freedom.

"Go, my servant, and do as you foresaw. Sow animosity and

fear into the Athenian hearts and minds. Prepare my way," Darius commanded. With a deep and solemn parting bow, Zahir left the king and crossed the waves to the city of Athens.

Once there, Zahir appeared as a shining being of living flame before a general from the Leontis tribe.

"Marathon!" Zahir declared in a voice as old as creation.

"Are you the mighty Apollo?" the general asked, his face filled with awe.

Zahir's flames rose higher. "Of course I am! Now, do as I say and take your men to Marathon!"

The general's name was Themistocles, and he defeated Darius's army at Marathon so thoroughly that it drove the king of kings mad with the shame of it. When he died soon after, and his body was covered with wax, it was as a broken man.

When asked, Zahir had always argued that his prophecy to Darius had been true. A great Persian king burned down Athens when Xerxes invaded some years later, and if Zahir hadn't appeared to Themistocles, it never would have happened.

This story revealed two very important warnings that one must heed for their own good.

The first was that to enslave a djinn was not the same as taming a dangerous creature. It merely invited him into your home so he could learn all the ways he could eventually use to destroy you.

The second was never, ever, fuck with Zahir the Eternal.

CHAPTER ONE

$\mathcal{I}$n the city of Florence, deep in a warehouse basement, Ezra Eliyahu swayed under the flashing blue and crimson lights. The music was pounding hard, and she was dancing, dancing, dancing. She needed this release like she needed her heartbeat. She had drunk considerably, and there was enough weed in the air that the week's stress dulled down and her good vibes amped up.

Raising a hand as she moved, Ezra sketched an invisible sigil in the air. Golden stars rained down from the ceiling, making the crowd cheer and gasp. Every star that landed on skin glowed, and magic sent a natural high through the party-goers' bloodstreams.

When you can do nothing else, you dance, her father's voice whispered to her through the music. She had always thought it was one of his nonsensical sayings, but as she got older and life got harder, she recognized the truth in it. Her life could be a total garbage fire, but she would head straight to the dance floor. Somehow, everything would turn out okay.

Ezra missed her father every day, but she couldn't bring herself to return to Venice. A few weeks before her twenty-eighth birthday, her mother, Lucia, had died, and for the two years afterward, Ezra and Judah had clung to each other in their grief. They had started doing magic together, and father and daughter had created wonders.

It had all gone wrong when her father made some new friends in a group of mages.

The Cabal of the Wise had creeped Ezra out from the minute Judah had mentioned them. She tried to warn him that they weren't to be trusted, that they were only out to use him. They had fought for the first time, and it ended when Ezra had packed her bags and left Venice. Six months, and neither one had reached out, both too angry and proud.

Don't think of it. Think of the music, Ezra told herself, the thorn still lodged in her heart. Blinking back her tears, she shouted a wordless sound amongst the music and noise and sent a bigger rain of magic over the crowd. It was a mere trick compared to what she could wield. It made people happy, and that was what she was paid for.

She had planned on using her degree in magio-history to work in some museum or academia. When she had gotten to Florence, her hopes had fallen apart, and she had ended up bartending before doing party tricks. It paid the bills. Her studies could wait. Everything could wait.

Two hours later, Ezra picked up her money that had been left at the bar and stepped out into the warm night. Summer was ending soon, and she wasn't looking forward to it. Heat made her blood and magic feel like it could flow properly.

Ezra had no fear of thieves or miscreants on her walk home to her apartment in Santo Spirito. She was more than adept at self-defense and kept a thin spike of a dagger in her boot at all times. When that failed, magic was always burning on her fingertips.

You are made for more than party tricks, Judah's voice echoed in the back of her head. Ezra knew it was true. She just didn't know what else to do with herself. She had thought Florence would inspire her magic and the power of creation. Ezra was uninspired to even pick up a pencil. Until she could get herself together enough to work on more complex sigil designs, the dance floor would have to do.

Ezra instantly spotted the man leaning against the wrought iron gate that led into her apartment building. It wasn't an unusual occurrence, but something about him made her wary. Under the glowing streetlamp, his pale eyes studied her.

"Excuse me, *signorina*. Are you Ezra Eliyahu?" he asked in a Veneto accent.

"Depends. Who is asking?" she replied, digging around her bag for her keys and slipping them between her fingers.

"I'm here representing your father's lawyer," he explained, taking a step toward her. "I'm sorry to tell you like this, but your father is dead, *signorina*."

Ezra stumbled, all thought of her safety vanishing as disbelief, anger, and shock hit her body all at once. She couldn't hear what the man was saying. His words were muffled as if he was talking underwater. She was still shaking her head when someone moved behind her. Sharp pain pierced her neck, and Ezra was out before she hit the ground.

CHAPTER TWO

*E*zra's eyes burned like someone had poured salt into them. She swore at the stinging pain in her neck and tried to sit up.

"I would go slowly if I were you, *signorina*," a voice said in the blurry darkness.

Ezra's vision started to clear. She was lying on a woven rug in a room crammed with books and papers. Notes, sigils, and sketches were tacked onto the walls. She could smell clay and magic and blood.

She finally recognized where she was, and her chest squeezed too tight. Her father's study.

They had taken her back to Venice.

"What the fuck did you people do to me?" she mumbled. "How long was I out?"

"About eighteen hours. A lot longer than I would've liked, but someone mixed up the dosage," the voice said. There was a rustle of movement, and a man came to stand in front of her. He was older than his voice, with gray through his hair and a gauntness about his face. He seemed vaguely familiar, but she didn't know from where.

"What do you want with me?" Ezra asked.

"Your father was working on something for us. We thought it was completed, but he deceived us." The man had the decency to look embarrassed.

Ezra laughed, even as her heart cracked with grief. "You are one of his Cabal, aren't you? I told him you would use him and cast him aside. I never thought that you would have the balls to kill him. He must've realized it too in the end and made sure that you would never succeed in your plans."

The man slapped her hard across the face, making her head rock back. It hurt, but it cleared the cobwebs away from her mind.

"We know you helped him create a golem. We saw it ourselves. You are the only one who knows how to complete his work. If you want to live, you will do it quickly. If you work with us, you will reap the rewards of that," he said, looming over her.

Ezra rubbed her face. "I don't know what you're talking about. We never made a golem. No one has made one since Prague in the 1600s."

The man pulled a small device from his pocket. It was a piece of magical artifice that captured moving images within a crystal and played them as a small projection.

He turned it on, and Ezra saw a smiling version of herself with her father. They were standing in front of a man made of clay. It was a beautiful creation that looked so lifelike. They had made it together, using magically infused clay and all of Ezra's creative skill.

She knew what was coming next, and her stomach dropped. Ezra hadn't known that her father had recorded that day.

In the projection, Judah waved a small scroll in the air and placed it in the golem's mouth. Magical lines of light streaked over the golem, and it shuddered to life.

The man turned the artifice off. "I need to know what was

on the scroll. The one that he gave us only brought our creature to life for a limited time. He fooled us into thinking that it was done."

"And you killed him before you realized. Why would you do that? He was helping you." Ezra reached for her magic, but it was silent in her veins. Whatever they had injected her with had dulled every one of her senses.

"He lacked a proper vision for the future," the man said.

"I know what it looks like on the crystal, but I don't know what he wrote on the scroll. I'm not an idiot. I know you are all powerful enough to get what you want from me. I can't give it to you because I don't know," Ezra said, giving him her most sincere expression.

The man crouched down beside her and placed his hands on her wrists. "I believe you can. We have all of Judah's paperwork, and you will unravel it."

Before Ezra could pull her hands away, the man spoke a word and black manacles appeared on her wrists. She didn't have time to contemplate their appearance because he uttered another word. The most agonizing pain she had ever experienced scorched her skin, and she screamed as the manacles melted into her and fused with her bones. The man let her go just as she fell forward and vomited on the floor.

"We won't be making the same mistake with you as we did with your father. You are bound to us, and nothing can break it. We know how strong your power is, so if you try to tamper with the bindings, they will kill you. Try to leave Venice, and they will kill you. Help us create life, and we will give you your own back." The man patted her on the head like she was an obedient dog. "We will be back in two days to check on your progress."

With that, he turned and walked out of the study and the house, the front door slamming behind him. Ezra was shaking and sweating in fear and fury. She was a slave.

* * *

WHEN SHE COULD FINALLY STAND, Ezra went to the kitchen for a cloth and cleaning gear and mopped up the vomit. She climbed up the stairs to her old room and pulled some clothes from the cupboard. Everything was how she left it six months ago, like Judah had been waiting for her return. Maybe if she hadn't been so proud, he would still be alive.

Ezra went into the bathroom, stripped off her clothes, and turned the shower on. Blessed hot water. She felt like vomiting again, so she sat on the cool tiles and put her head between her knees. She sobbed, a shaky, horrible sound of grief.

The drugs in her system were slowly wearing off, and she could feel the faintest tingle of warmth in her fingertips. She had never felt that powerless. The shock of it was hitting her, and she couldn't stop shaking.

Ezra had been so proud the day they first got the golem to move. They were descendants of Rabbi Judah Loew ben Bezalel, the famous Maharal of Prague, and making golems was in their blood. It had started as a fun project with Judah after her mother had died. It had been something to turn their minds to and puzzle out. Both Ezra and Judah were better when they were busy.

If she had known that the Cabal would try to get Judah to make more golems, she wouldn't have dared leave Venice. Her father had been lonely, but she had never imagined that he would tell anyone about their experiments. They knew as soon as they had created it that it could be used for deadly force. They had destroyed the scroll and had boxed up the clay man.

What had convinced Judah to try again? What had they promised him? Ezra had to find answers. She couldn't let the Cabal get away with murdering her father.

Ezra rubbed her wrists. She let her magic softly brush against the bindings under her skin. Black marks rose to the

11

surface like tattoos. They were starting to burn when she released her magic, then they disappeared once more. She had to find out what her father had been working on. She didn't think golems would have been enough for the Cabal to want to kill him.

Depends on what they were going to use them for.

Once Ezra was in dry clothes and the world stopped swaying, she went back downstairs and made a strong coffee. Her father mustn't have been dead long because the kitchen still had edible food in it. She didn't know where his body had been taken. Had they buried him already? Had anyone done rites over him? Said words?

"Focus on what you can control now. Grieve later," she growled at herself. She wasn't going to get revenge for her father's murder if she fell apart.

Coffee in hand, Ezra went back into the study and started going through the papers scattered on the walls. Judah had a wild, creative, unstoppable mind when he was fixated on a project. It was one thing they had in common. A small sketch on the corner of a grocery bill caught her attention. It was an urn with a sigil on the side of it. It had no power in it, only a scribble to represent the magic that would go in its place. There was a line of Judah's writing underneath, so messy, it was almost unreadable.

Infused clay will hold them with a powerful enough sigil. Ask Ezra.

Ice filled Ezra's belly. She remembered her mother telling her magical fairy tales about the djinn when she was small. Tales where they had been captured in bottles and were able to grant wishes that always backfired. She looked at the sketch again and realized what it was. A prison for a djinn.

"Oh, Papa, tell me you didn't..." she whispered. Judah had a deep mistrust of the djinn, but this wasn't like him. He believed all beings should be free.

But you know what he is like when someone gives him a problem.

Or what he was *like.* His mind couldn't help trying to solve it. He often referred to the compulsion as a curse because he couldn't stop it once it started. If the Cabal had proposed such a prison in passing, presented it as a hypothetical thought study to Judah...

Ezra felt like crying again, but she swallowed the salt in her mouth and tried to think. She was powerful, but the slave spell wouldn't let her magic anywhere near it, and she couldn't run away. She couldn't give the Cabal any help with their golems or clay djinn traps. They would kill her if she didn't. They had already proved they were capable of it

Ezra was smart enough to know she needed help. She had to find someone in Venice who was strong enough to take on, not only the spell, but the Cabal as well.

One name was at the top of her list. A chill swept through her as she considered it.

Judah hadn't had many rules for her growing up. There were only two that he continued to warn her against as she got older. Never make a deal with a djinn, and never speak the name of Zahir the Eternal, in case he comes to find you.

Ezra didn't have to speak his name. She knew exactly where to find the King of the Djinn.

CHAPTER THREE

There were days that Zahir truly resented his decision to sit on the Council of Ten. The Ten ruled all the Republic from the powerful seat of Venice, and they made sure that anyone—shape changer, mage, djinn, or normal human— was welcome. If you obeyed the rules and worshiped trade above all else, there was no finer place to live.

The djinn loved bureaucracy. They excelled at it, so Zahir resented not enjoying himself far more with the intricacies of running the Republic. The truth was, he was bored down to the bones he didn't really have. The war with the magic hating Varangian Empire seemed to be never-ending, and his days were filled with endless meetings like the one he was currently trapped in.

Zahir was doing his best to focus on the dashingly handsome Admiral Nico D'Argento and the report he was giving the council. It was an update on new ship designs that could help them in the war. There was a brilliant artifice mage in Constantinople who had taken old engine designs and had begun to create something similar that used magic to power it. It was going to be far more powerful and efficient than the current magical batteries. Nico wanted to bring him to Venice and give him more funding to expand the experiment to one of his warships.

Zahir could remember when petrol had powered such things, and he had vowed to ensure that nothing so filthy contaminated the atmosphere. Humans had fucked the world once, and he wasn't about to let it happen again.

Zahir glanced over to Arkon's notebook. The sorcerer beside him was busily drawing a picture of the Wolf Mage with devil horns and a pitchfork. Arkon was perhaps the closest thing he had to a friend, and his mind was only ever on one thing.

Every day that the Wolf Mage evaded capture, or assassination, was another day Arkon was planning to take her down. He had gotten more gray in his hair in recent months. He had far too much for a man so young.

Zahir felt a twinge of something that could have been concern. He pushed it aside. If the djinn knew one thing, it was not to get attached to humans. They were fragile little butterflies that died too young.

"We still haven't uncovered what the Varangians wanted with our unregistered magic users," Gio said, his deep voice bringing Zahir back to the present. The former had curly dark hair and eyes that could strip you bare with a glance. Zahir only ever saw them soften when Gio talked to one person—Carmella Aladoro. The female shedu shapeshifter in question was the leader of the Wands District, along with her son Domenico.

They had all rescued a shipload of their own people that winter, thanks to Domenico and his lovely mate, Stella. Carmella was the kindest of people right up until you crossed her. Zahir had seen what had been left of her late husband and knew that he would never dare to get on her bad side.

The Varangians hadn't gotten their hands on the Republic's stolen mages. That they wanted them at all still made no sense. They hated magic, except for their blessed Wolf Mage.

Gio cleared his throat and said louder, "Where are your Ravens at with that, Arkon?"

Zahir gave the Grand Sorcerer and spy master a helpful kick under the table.

"Ah, um, yes. The Ravens." Arkon flipped through his notebook, pretending he was looking for information. The entire book was filled with his sketches of the Wolf Mage in varying gory deaths. "They traced the last shipload of unregistered magic users to Sarajevo. There, the trail went cold. My informant believes they were handed over to the army and shipped off to a camp. They couldn't find anything reliable to corroborate that and have headed to Kyiv to see if the Wolf Mage might be training them or using them for something...else."

Zahir knew when his friend was holding back, but the council meetings weren't the place for actual information. Gio and Arkon had their own agreements, Zahir knew it, and so did anyone with half a brain in the Republic. They attended the Council of Ten for the day to day. The things that occurred in the night were for them alone.

"Keep me informed, and let's continue to look at changing the registration policies to encourage other unlisted users to come forward," Gio replied smoothly. He raised a slight brow at Arkon, and the sorcerer nodded. They would talk later.

After the meeting was finally over, Zahir looped his arm around Arkon's before he could go anywhere. The sorcerer had an uncanny knack for disappearing after meetings.

"Before you ask, I can't come drinking with you tonight," Arkon said before Zahir could open his mouth.

"I wasn't going to, though you seem in dire need of a drink. Tell me what's wrong, my dear sorcerer," Zahir replied. It was a sunny afternoon, and they walked along the marble mezzanine that looked over St. Mark's Square.

"The Wolf Mage is what is wrong. Just like always," Arkon admitted, running a hand through his already messy curls.

They stopped to lean against the railings and stare at the glittering blue ocean. It was a sight Zahir never tired of although it still frightened many of his brethren. He loved the sea. If he ever decided to kill himself, he would throw himself into the dark blue waters and let them unmake him.

"What has she done now that has you so vexed, Arkon?" Zahir prompted him.

"That's the thing. I don't think she's done anything. The attacks on our soldiers recently aren't her," Arkon struggled to explain.

"She's their only mage."

"Is she? Because I know this magic looks like her, but it's not. The last report said that she tore horses and men apart. Some were reported to be inside out. That's horrific."

"That's war."

Arkon shook his head. "Not our war. The Wolf Mage isn't the slaughtering type. Her magic is subtle."

"Sending a plague of mice onto our military encampment isn't subtle," Zahir argued.

"It is fair, though. Magic should never be used to kill. There's balance and a natural law that it defies. You know this better than anyone. Besides, I turned the mice into potatoes and fed the men for a month." Arkon leaned against the railing. "These attacks we have been seeing in the past month are not her doing."

"Maybe you are only hoping that they're not," Zahir suggested softly.

Arkon's expression turned fierce. "What do you mean by that?"

"She's your rival and your equal, Arkon. You two have played a game of magical chess with each other for years. You respect her, and you think you know her. You don't. You play by a code of honor, but you can't expect her to do the same."

17

Arkon gnawed on his lip. "She has up until now. What has changed?"

"She answers to her masters. Maybe they are forcing her hand. The king might want this war over by any means necessary," Zahir suggested. He didn't want to upset the sorcerer more, but he wouldn't lie to him either. "I'm sure your Ravens will find something. They always do."

"I don't know what to do, Zahir," Akron admitted, his dark brown eyes worried. "Gio wants me to respond in kind, to show the king and his mage that we aren't to be fucked with. I don't think I can do it. Just because she is willing to kill with magic doesn't mean I can. Not even for Gio."

Zahir thought about the horrible position the sorcerer was in. He knew what it was like to have a master. "How about a freak snowstorm?" he suggested eventually.

Arkon's mouth twitched. "I like it. Powerful. Uncomfortable. It will give the men a fighting chance, at least. If any die, the blame will bounce back onto the king for not equipping his army as he should. Has anyone ever told you that you would make an excellent advisor?"

Zahir laughed, a rich sound that had heads turning. "I only give advice when I feel like it. I only give *good* advice if I like you."

"There is another possibility that I have to consider where these recent attacks are concerned," Arkon said, his mirth vanishing.

"And what is that?"

"That perhaps the Varangians have stopped killing their magicians and have started training them to be obedient soldiers of the empire."

Zahir gave Arkon's shoulder a squeeze. "The Creator help us all if that's the case. The Wolf Mage alone has vexed you enough."

"I just need to kill her, and everything will be fine," Arkon said decisively.

"That's the spirit." Not that that plan had worked so far. "You need any help to put together a decent weather spell?"

"Don't insult me," Arkon said, batting Zahir's hand from his arm. "Don't you have petitioners to attend to?"

Zahir sighed. "Don't remind me."

"I won't keep you from your duties, Highness," Arkon said, his sly grin finally making an appearance.

"Enjoy making snow flurries for your girlfriend," Zahir countered, and he headed for the stairs.

CHAPTER FOUR

stunningly beautiful female djinn was waiting for
Zahir outside of the palace walls. Her hair was a mass
of braids, threaded with lapis lazuli beads, and she wore a gold
and blue kaftan. She looked like the ancient queen she had been
so long ago. Ashirah was smoking something that smelled of
blue lotus and cinnamon. It was an ageless blend from Egypt
that djinn adored, and his second in command was no different.

"What's wrong with the sorcerer?" Ashirah asked as he fell
into step beside her. People in the square stared at them. Zahir
was used to it. They both could make themselves incorporeal,
but sometimes it was important to be seen.

"The Wolf Mage, like always."

"Maybe you should transport him to Kyiv so he can fuck her.
It might help him get her out of his system," Ashirah replied,
ever the pragmatist.

"Unfortunately, Arkon getting laid wouldn't be much use to
the Republic."

She blew out a fragrant cloud of smoke. "It will if he stabs
her after he's done."

Zahir's laughter bubbled out of him. "You're so romantic."

"All my dead husbands would disagree with you," she replied with a wicked grin.

Zahir's boat was docked in a special space reserved for council members. He didn't usually bother to bring it with him. He had been in a mood that morning, and he wanted home close.

When Zahir was struck with boredom, like the current malaise affecting him, he liked to be on the water. It reminded him that he could still die and that he wasn't quite ready to face that fate yet. Life always seemed to find a way to surprise him out of taking the final leap overboard. He just had to hang on long enough for it to happen.

Zahir went into his cabin and sat behind the cluttered wooden desk. "Take us home," he told the boat. On deck, the ropes untied themselves from their moorings, and the ship drifted away from the dock. It would go wherever it knew that petitioners were, and it was never wrong.

Ashirah watched him carefully from her place under the porthole window. She hummed a little. "You're not yourself today."

"What are you, my wife?"

"Like I'd be stupid enough to marry the likes of you. Out with it, old friend. I know something is wrong."

Zahir pulled at one of the golden hoops in his ears. "I feel like my fire has gone out."

"You're a djinn. Your fire can't go out. You could make all of Gio's dreams come true and go and stop the war single-handedly," Ashirah suggested.

"I have no appetite for killing half frozen soldiers. You know the rules: if we interfere like that, the humans will fear us. I want us to have a place in this new world. Besides, I have seen what men do when they have a weaponized djinn. I wouldn't follow Gio if I didn't trust him, but some things are better left in the past and forgotten," Zahir replied. He felt terribly ancient all of a sudden.

"Take a lover. Take ten if you have to. You will find something amongst them to keep you interested and occupied," Ashirah said impatiently.

Zahir leaned back in his chair and stared at the wooden ceiling. "Even that doesn't seem like a challenge anymore."

"You have petitioners to see and their problems to solve," Ashirah snapped and lit another smoke. "Pull yourself together and stop being pathetic."

Zahir chuckled. "I love you too, my sister."

"Bah. Pathetic like all males," Ashirah repeated.

They had barely pulled into the dock when the first petitioner scrambled on deck. Zahir looked pleadingly at Ashirah. "Make me tea?"

Another petitioner hit the deck. It was going to be one of those days.

"I'll make it strong," she said and disappeared, leaving streaks of indigo smoke in the air.

Someone knocked on the door, and Zahir let his face settle into his feared King of the Djinn pose. "Enter," he boomed and got ready for more boredom.

* * *

IN ZAHIR'S long life of granting humans their hearts' desires, he had learned that they basically boiled down to three things— money, power, and love. He could smell the desperation on the gamblers, see the pining in the eyes of the besotted. Usually, he could ignore it, make the best deal, and send grateful wretches on their way.

"Stop. I've had enough," he begged the magic of the boat. He was done.

It was sunset, and an entourage of djinn that acted as bodyguards had already established themselves on the deck of the boat. They were smoking a hookah and lounging on silken pillows.

Zahir wanted to hear all about the magical and wonderful things they had seen and created that day. He was king, and so he couldn't walk amongst the Wands District as openly as he liked. His djinn had to do it for him.

Ashirah came into the cabin with another pot of tea—his third—and caught him with his head on the desk.

"Tsk. You are in a bad way today," she said, putting the tea down.

Zahir groaned. His magic twitched irritably under his skin, rippling through him like a tidal wave. He rubbed at his arms as flames danced out of his skin. Something was wrong...

Feet hit the deck of the boat.

"I need to speak with the king," a woman's voice echoed through the door. She shouldn't have been able to get on deck at all after he closed for the day.

He looked through the window of the door that was invisible from the outside. Asim's tall body was blocking the woman's path, and Zahir couldn't see her. Zahir's magic flared again, like a warning of danger.

"The king isn't in. Please wait until he's open to petitioners once more," the huge djinn said, his deep voice unyielding. A look from Asim was usually enough to dissuade someone from arguing.

"I can feel his magic radiating through this boat. I know he's here. Move aside," the woman demanded.

Ashirah chuckled. "We have a lively one tonight. I bet you two *soldi* that Asim tosses her into the canal."

"I'll take that bet," Zahir replied, his power dancing over his skin once more. What the hell was going on?

"*Signorina*, please don't make me use force. You are trespassing," Asim growled. He moved aside, and Zahir got a look at the firebrand. She was short, barely coming up to the center of Asim's chest, with generous curves of hips and breasts. Her hair was a thick abundance of dark curls around a face that was pure fury. Zahir felt a stirring of interest mix in with his erratic magic. He had a weakness for passionate women.

The stranger smiled suddenly at Asim, beautiful and open. "You know what? Why don't you go and play with your friends?" she suggested. She pointed at them, wiggling a finger in the air.

Zahir put a hand on the door, ready to intervene, when the strangest thing happened. Golden sparkles began to fall on the djinn. Asim tilted his face up to them, and a dopey smile spread across his face.

"You're right. We shouldn't be fighting. You can join us if you like," he said with a charming smile designed to drop panties wherever he aimed it.

The woman patted him on the arm. "Maybe after I see the king, we can hang out."

"I'd like that. So pretty," Asim replied, touching a dark red curl buried amongst all the black.

Ashirah sucked in a surprised breath. "What the fuck just happened to him?"

"I have no idea. Let's see if she can get past the wards on the door," Zahir said. He sat behind his desk and hastily finger combed his hair. He had never seen anyone able to enchant a djinn before and didn't want her to try it on him.

Ashirah took up her usual seat and poured herself a cup of tea. "You're not bored now, are you?"

Zahir's magic flared as the woman touched the door. He could feel her magic, subtle and powerful and unlike anything he'd experienced before in a human. The sound of her laughing came through the wood, deep and husky. It was a sound made for the bedroom, and Zahir wanted to hear it again. She tore the ward free and barged through the door with a kick of her black combat boots.

"I'm here to see the King of the Djinn," she declared, her breathing heavy. Her dark, kohl-rimmed eyes were burning with power.

Wow, look at you. Zahir fought to keep a bored expression. "And you've found him. What do you want, rude girl?"

"It's Ezra, not rude girl. Ezra Eliyahu." She took a breath and dared to look him dead in the eyes. "I need your help."

"Your kind always does. What with?" Zahir poured himself more tea, preparing for something mundane. It would be a waste after such a fun entry.

"With this," Ezra said and lifted her arms. She had pretty tattoos decorating her ringed fingers and slender wrists. Her magic let out a low hum and marks rose on her skin. Zahir put his tea down on the desk before he dropped it. He strode over to her, but Ezra didn't move. Her brow furrowed in pain.

Zahir took her hands in his. He knew the magic that bound her. The enslaving spells were highly illegal in the Republic, and they were hurting her by just revealing them to him.

Zahir's grip on her tightened, and flames filled his eyes. Fury made his voice deepen. "Who the fuck did this to you?"

CHAPTER FIVE

*E*zra had never possessed the deep distrust and fear of the djinn that her father had, but standing before Zahir the Eternal was taking every ounce of courage she had. If she hadn't had her anger sustaining her, she doubted she would have stepped onto his boat at all.

Zahir was not what she expected. He was handsome in a shocking way that felt like a punch knocking the air out of her. He was dressed in black tailored pants and a burned orange collared shirt. His thick, dark hair was brushed back from a brown, bearded face. He had a full smirking mouth; gold glinted in his ears, and a scent rose from him like desert sand and spice. He still held onto her wrists, flames flickering in his dark eyes. Her mouth went bone dry at the anger in them.

"Who the fuck did this to you?" he growled out. The threat in his voice robbed her of some of her courage.

"I-I don't know his name. He was part of a group called the Cabal of the Wise. They killed my father," Ezra said. She let her magic go with a gasp, the burning of the marks becoming too much. The bindings faded away. Zahir's thumbs stroked over her skin, leaving traces of heat that made her heart race.

26

"Sit," he commanded, gesturing to the chair opposite the desk. Ezra sat, all the adrenaline leaving her shaky. Zahir passed her a steaming glass cup of mint tea.

Ezra was so confused by the gesture, she had a sip without thinking. It was warm and fragrant, and it calmed the nausea in her stomach.

Zahir leaned against the table and crossed his arms. They were impressive arms, she noticed, and then hated herself. The djinn were all so beautiful that desire was never far behind.

"You had best start from the beginning," Zahir said, his deep voice charming once more.

Ezra took another sip of her tea and glanced at the other djinn sitting in the corner of the room. She didn't need an introduction. *Ashirah.*

Ezra had grown up with rumors that she was the actual lost goddess of the Jews who had once been the consort of the god El, father of the gods, before a lower war god in the pantheon, Yahweh, had stolen her away and overthrown El. She had also been a consort to Solomon and a queen in Egypt. The tales spun on.

"You can trust me, little one," Ashirah said, reading the worry that Ezra hadn't voiced aloud.

Ezra licked her lips. "It started just after my mother died..." She told them about the golem, their argument about the new friends her father had made, their fight, her kidnapping, and his murder.

Zahir frowned. "They want you to make golems? That magic has been lost for centuries. Why, the last time was... God, I can't remember."

"Prague. 1600s," Ezra said.

"Exactly. What made them certain that you could do it?" Zahir asked, giving her a sceptical once over.

"They have a projection of the night my father and I achieved it."

Ashirah clicked her tongue. "You are a descendent of the Maharal of Prague, aren't you?"

"Yes. My father and I tried to recreate his magic, and we succeeded. We didn't expect it to work. When it did, we realized what we had done. We destroyed the scroll, the *shem* that gave it life, and we boxed the golem up." Ezra felt like she was betraying Judah's memory just by being there and divulging their secrets. She pushed the feeling down. He had done the same by telling the Cabal about her.

"And now this Cabal… They killed him without checking the magic and want you to fix it?" Zahir said.

"Yes. I'm bound to them until I finish it. I can't break the spell on my own."

Zahir inspected his nails. "You broke into here fine. I'm sure a clever girl like you will be able to figure it out."

"You won't help me?" Ezra demanded.

"I don't know why I should. I have no jurisdiction in the Jewish Quarter that you are a part of. That's the Doge's problem, so he is the one you should be petitioning," Zahir replied calmly.

Ezra's eyes narrowed. "That's not the real reason."

"Well, you haven't told me the truth, have you?"

"How could you know that?" Ezra asked. Her heart was beating hard, but she tried to keep the panic from her face. She had told him the truth, just not all of it.

Zahir's eyes sparked with flames as he leaned into her space. "The sparrow does not come to the lion for help to deal with yapping dogs. So what is it about this Cabal that scares you more than me, little bird?"

"Apart from the fact they have *enslaved* me and want me to make unstoppable warriors for them?" she asked incredulously.

Zahir studied her face carefully. "Yes."

"I… I have reason to suspect that they want to entrap djinn," Ezra whispered, unable to look away from him.

The flames in his eyes were so bright now, they appeared gold. "Your proof?"

"The Cabal hates the djinn. They think you have too much power and that you're abominations of the Creator. It was one of the many things I argued about with my father." Ezra reached into her bra and pulled out the sketch. "I found this in my father's study."

Zahir took the paper and unfolded it. He went still. "Keep talking."

Ezra spun her theory out to him that her father could have been influenced by the Cabal to create such a thing.

"What does he mean here by 'Ask Ezra?' Why would you be the key to such a prison?"

Ezra lifted her chin. "I'll tell you if you promise not to kill me."

"Don't take that deal, Zahir," Ashirah said, looking at the sketch over his shoulder.

Ezra tried to be brave, but it wasn't working. She was exhausted, hung over from whatever poison she had been injected with, and so filled with grief, she wanted to tear Venice apart.

"If we kill her, we will never find this Cabal," Zahir said. He turned his attention back to Ezra. "I promise not to kill you. Now answer me."

"My magic is creation. Specifically, sigil creation. I could, in theory, create a seal that would be able to trap a djinn in magically infused clay," she said and waited for the blow. Neither djinn moved.

"What makes you certain you have the power to affect a djinn? We are made of magic, after all," Zahir said.

"Did you not see how high your djinn are out on deck? That's a party spell of mine. An easy child's trick, really," Ezra replied, trying to sound as cocky as he did.

"Kill her. Or I will," Ashirah hissed, a curved blade appearing in her hand.

"No. I made a promise. We need to find this Cabal, especially if they are building golems. There're only two reasons they want them—to use them against the djinn or sell them to the Varangians. If we kill her, we lose our only lead," Zahir argued. He stared at her without saying anything. Ashirah huffed and went and sat back in her corner.

Ezra sipped her tea as the silence in the cabin stretched on. If they did kill her, it would be better than being a slave. She wasn't good with pain, and the bindings would be used to torture her until she did what they wanted. They would get it from her, eventually. She closed her eyes and waited for her death.

CHAPTER SIX

*Z*ahir studied the strange creature before him. He had wanted life to become more interesting, but not *this* kind of interesting. This was a powder keg of problems ready to explode in his face.

A human woman powerful enough to trap djinn and make golems. He hadn't seen that kind of power for thousands of years. Ashirah was right; he should kill her for all their safety. The problem was this woman's strange magic not only sparked against his; it made it burn inside of him like a damn inferno. He wanted to know why.

"Here is my offer," Zahir said finally. "You will work for me as a spy to uncover the members of this Cabal. When you have enough information for me to act on, I will take the information to the Doge and have them arrested. Only when they are stopped, will I remove the bindings from you."

"You are making me serve them? Are you insane?" Ezra demanded.

"Probably. I still need to know what they are up to. Your father managed to fool them. I'm sure you will have no problems doing the same. You had best work quickly on finding out their identities, hmm?" he said, unable to resist goading her.

Ezra's chin lifted. "Anything else?"

Zahir went to say no, but his mouth said, "I demand three nights with you. When and where will be of my choosing."

Ashirah choked on her tea behind him.

"Three nights doing what?" Ezra asked.

"Whatever the fuck I like."

"Why?"

Now, wasn't that the real question? Zahir shrugged. "Because you hate djinn, and this kind of deal requires a sacrifice on your behalf. In this case, it's your pride."

"And I won't be harmed physically during these nights? I'm not trading one torturer for another," Ezra said. She was clever enough to ask.

"Of course you won't be harmed, but I can't say the same for my feelings. I'm a little offended that you would put me on the level of slavers," Zahir replied angrily.

"I find out who the Cabal is and spend three nights with you, and you take these bindings off me and don't kill me and neither do any of your djinn," she summarized. Ezra surprised him with the last part. She knew he couldn't kill once a bargain was struck, but that didn't mean he couldn't get someone else to do the deed.

Clever and fierce and almost oozing magic. What a combination.

Zahir saw the indecision dash through her eyes. He couldn't let her walk away. He leaned down until they were almost nose to nose. "What's the matter, sparrow? Are you scared of me?" he teased.

"Only a fool wouldn't be," she whispered. She bit her full bottom lip, and he suddenly wanted to know what it tasted like. Ezra's eyes fixed on him and narrowed. "Fine. I agree to your deal, but if they kill me before I can find the information for you, I will haunt you for all eternity."

"Then you will be in excellent company with all my other enemies," Zahir replied. He held out a hand. Ezra took it and shook. The magic of the deal danced between them, and three small black strokes appeared on her arm like a tally.

"It's done," Zahir said.

Ezra released his hand first and tugged it back. She got to her feet, forcing him to lean back.

"I live in the Ghetto Nuovo. If you want updates, that's where you will find me."

Zahir frowned. "You don't want to give me your phone number?"

"I don't have one. Too expensive, and they are a good excuse for someone to rob you. You want information, you'll figure out how to get it to me. I won't risk my life coming to the djinn again," Ezra said. She gave Zahir a final once over before she walked out of the office and slammed the door behind her.

"That was a mistake," Ashirah said, getting up to pace. "You should have listened to me and killed her."

Zahir was still staring at the door, suddenly hating that the strange woman was gone. "That's the benefit of being king. I don't have to listen to anyone."

"And the three nights?" she demanded. "There are prettier women in the city, willing to spread their legs for you.

Zahir shrugged. "She doesn't like djinn. I didn't think she would agree to it."

"You let her leave when she has the potential to entrap us."

Zahir let out a frustrated sigh. "But she won't. She doesn't hate us that much or she wouldn't have come here at all."

Ashirah shook her head at him. "You are out of your mind."

"Wouldn't be for the first time. I'm going to see where she goes next," Zahir said and melted into the ether before she could talk him out of it.

It was freeing to be out of the confines of a physical body. He shot out of the cabin, sparing a glance to the high djinn on deck. Asim was staring at his hands like he'd never seen them before. Whatever she had hit them with must have been good.

Zahir followed the trail of magic that Ezra had left behind her. It was an intoxicating coppery haze that made his magic tingle. What strange power did she have? Sigil magic was common, but he didn't believe that was what she had. Any magician could draw a sigil. It was the magic behind them that created the effectiveness. She could draw them in the air without any other tool. It was something that went so far beyond a simple sigil ability.

Zahir found Ezra buying food and wine at a small bistro in the Campo del Ghetto Nuovo. The owners seemed to recognize her because they hugged her and gave her condolences about her father. Ezra accepted the bags of food, crossed the square, and let herself into a townhouse. It was three stories high and had plants hanging from window boxes.

So this is home. Zahir whispered a revealing word, and the house lit up with warding. Impressive. Complicated. Ezra's power mixed in with something else which must've been her father's magical signature.

A door opened on the second-floor balcony, and she appeared. She stared right where he stood. Zahir froze. There was no way she could see him.

But can she sense you? He had no idea, and it sent a thrill through him.

Ezra stared a little longer before shaking her head and going back inside.

It took a lot to rattle Zahir, but she had shaken him to his core. "What in all the hells are you, Ezra Eliyahu?"

CHAPTER SEVEN

*T*he Eliyahu house had always been a chaotic mess of a scholar's den. The kitchen and bathrooms were generally the only rooms that were kept clean and free of the cluttered piles of books, papers, and notebooks.

Ezra sat on the Turkish carpets in her father's study, a bowl of steaming risotto on one knee and a scattering of papers in front of her.

"What were you up to?" she mumbled to herself.

To take her mind off her deal with the djinn, Ezra had started to go through her father's study. It was even messier than she remembered. She scooped another mouthful of creamy risotto into her mouth and tried to ignore the sorrow throbbing in her chest. It hurt to be back in the family house and surrounded by so many memories. She missed her parents and their advice on what to do about her situation.

They would have told you to stay the hell away from the djinn for a start, she mused.

Ezra didn't know what to expect from Zahir the Eternal. She knew from gossip that his presence was overwhelming. She had thought that was only a story. She should have known better.

Being in Zahir's presence was like standing next to the sun. He radiated so much magic that Ezra was surprised he could contain it. He hadn't blown up all of Venice on any of his bad days, but that didn't mean he wasn't capable of it.

Ezra's eyes drifted to the three dark marks on her arm. Three nights with a djinn. What the hell had she been thinking? She hadn't been. She had wanted his help and was desperate enough to agree to whatever he wanted. Three nights with Zahir. Doing what? She had no idea and hadn't asked for specifics. Her skin heated with a flush of warmth.

Zahir was unnaturally attractive. He radiated sex and desire. He no doubt made sure of it because he wanted to beguile and dazzle whoever visited him. Humans were unnaturally drawn to beauty. It was a fatal flaw that the djinn knew how to exploit.

Ezra shook her head. She doubted Zahir wanted her for sex when his escapades were numerous and his reputation outstripped Venice's other notorious lover, Casanova.

Her magic was a strange thing at the best of times, but it seemed to burn hotter in Zahir's presence. Not only that, but she could have *sworn* she felt him following her earlier. There had been no sign of any djinn at all. Just her mind playing tricks on her.

One visit to the djinn, and you're already going mad.

Ezra finished her risotto, placed the empty bowl on a coffee table, and went to sit at Judah's desk. There were still smears of clay and blood on some of the pages. Awareness rippled over her. Had he died in this very place? Her eyes went to the family portrait on the desk, splattered with blood. It had been taken before Lucia had died, and it was the last picture they had, all of them smiling.

In the protective glass over the picture, Ezra's drawn face reflected back to her and the bookshelf behind her. Something twinkled in the corner of her eye, and she whirled around.

Nestled in between copies of the *Zohar* and *The Emerald*

Tablet was a piece of a dark chunk of crystal about the size of her pinkie finger. Ezra pulled it free. It had a small scroll wrapped around it that said, *Ezra's bat mitzvah.*

She frowned, turning it over in her hand. She had never had a bat mitzvah. Ezra's mother had been raised Catholic, and her father had been Jewish. Neither one of them had been religious enough to force her to do any ceremonies for either faith. If they had worshipped anything, it had been magic, history, and knowledge.

Ezra dug through the desk and found the artifice device that the crystal slotted into. Images flicked to life in the air above it. They were of designs and sigils, golems being crafted, a man speaking about a contact called Ingvar Hardrada and a delivery.

"You were already gathering information on them," Ezra murmured. Judah's face flickered in front of her. He looked like he'd aged years in the six months that they had been apart.

"If they kill me, you have to stop them, Ezra. I didn't know what they truly planned to use the golems for. They funded me and told me they would use them for the good of Venice. I thought they meant to help with construction or to protect the city. Don't listen to them! They lie and lie and lie. You were right. I should've never joined them," Judah said, his speech more erratic than ever. Whatever they had done to him had broken him, reducing him to madness.

"Oh, Papa," Ezra whispered.

"They are going to sell them to the Varangians. There's some deal they have going on with one of the nobles. He promised to rid Venice of the djinn for them in exchange for unstoppable warriors. Don't let them capture you. They will use your magic until there's nothing left. I love—"

The recording cut off, and Ezra put the device down before she smashed it against the wall.

Hot tears that she had been holding back rolled down her

cheeks. Ezra covered her face, smothering her scream into her palms. She should never have left Judah alone.

After a while, Ezra wiped at her cheeks and took some deep breaths. Zahir was right. They needed to find out the identities of the men in the Cabal. This was all so much bigger than Judah's murder.

The Cabal might believe the Varangians would get rid of the djinn from Venice, but Ezra knew it was impossible. No one had enough power to do that. Not even if the Wolf Mage herself commanded an army of golems. The Varangians would use them to expand their empire, eradicating magic as they went.

Ezra removed the crystal from the device. She found a ball of silver wire in Judah's supply cabinet and wrapped it around the crystal, making it look like a harmless pendant, and strung it on the silver chain around her neck. She couldn't risk leaving it where one of the Cabal could find it. They had already proven that they could get through the house's wards any time they wished.

Ezra found a notebook and sketched out the sigil she had seen on the crystal. It was so different from what her father usually created, and it wasn't the same *shem* design they had made together. He wouldn't have put it on the crystal if it wasn't important, so she had no choice but to try to figure out what it did. She also needed to come up with something fake to feed the Cabal while she tried to uncover their identities for Zahir.

Ezra drained the last of her wine before she put on coffee. She had a feeling the convoluted puzzle Judah had left her wasn't going to be easy to unravel.

CHAPTER EIGHT

Zahir wasn't a fan of mysteries that weren't of his own making. The day after Ezra's visit to his boat, Zahir sent people to watch over her and gather everything there was to know about her. Ezra Eliyahu wouldn't be a mystery for long. He would make sure of it. He would know what made her tick, what food she liked, what kind of present would entice favor.

Are you watching her or courting her? He didn't know the answer to that. A part of him wanted to hang her upside down by her feet and demand to know what it was about her that made him so damn curious.

"Have they found anything useful yet?" Zahir asked Ashirah irritably. Technically, she was in charge of his network of spies and informants.

"Depends on what you are classifying as useful, my king," she replied. She had been full of sass about the girl ever since he'd made the deal. She always knew when he was hiding something, but in this case, he didn't know what it was.

"Everything. I want to know everything," he said. They were in one of his houses in Cannaregio, and he was pacing a track on the soft carpets.

"I'll start at the beginning, shall I?" Ashirah produced a small notebook from thin air and opened it. "Ezra Eliyahu, born of Judah and Lucia. Both of her parents were magio-historians, and she has a degree in it herself. Whatever that is."

Zahir toyed with his thumb ring. "They study old spells and magical processes and figure out which ones work and which ones don't. They can revive old magic."

"I suppose that explains why they attempted to create golems from the Maharal's writings. It was probably their idea of a fun experiment," Ashirah said and referred back to her notebook. "Ezra's mother, Lucia, died of cancer a few years ago. According to gossip, Ezra had a fight with Judah about six or seven months ago, and she went to live in Florence. She has a small apartment there and was making money with the clubs, performing her magical highs, much like the one she threw at Asim and the others."

Zahir didn't like the sound of that. "Do you think others know what kind of magic she has? That she can bewitch djinn?"

"I doubt it, my king. If it was known, I'm sure some enthusiastic patron would have snatched her up by now. Sigil magic like hers isn't completely unique. She might not have felt the need to hide it at all."

"I need to be sure. I'll go and talk to Arkon today and see what his Ravens know," Zahir said, rubbing his chin. "If they knew about her, I'm sure he would've recruited her."

Ashirah raised a brow. "Maybe he has. She could be one of his flock."

"She better not be," Zahir grumbled.

"Why? What is it exactly about this girl that has you so intrigued? She's not overly beautiful, at least not in the way you prefer."

"It's not about that." Zahir lied. It wasn't *only* about that. "It's something I can't quite put my finger on. It's like she's something I have forgotten and can't remember. Like a scratch on my brain. She smells like myrrh, magic, and mystery. I have to figure her out."

Ashirah let out a small sigh. "If you say so. Anything else you require?"

"Yes. I want her watched at all times. Put two guards on her. I want to know who is coming in and out of that house."

"What about if she has a lover?" Ashirah asked.

Zahir's eyes narrowed. He didn't like that idea but nodded. "Yes, I suppose I better know that too. We can't have her pillow talking about the Cabal and alerting that we are onto them. She needs to be guarded. She's under my protection."

"Is she now? That's news."

Zahir waved an irritated hand. "Yes, yes, of course she is. It's a part of the deal."

"Hmm, must've been in the fine print," Ashirah mused.

Zahir frowned at her. "She was brave enough to come to us for help, and she's acting as a spy to uncover this conspiracy. We have to protect her. She's an asset."

"Of course, my king. I'll find some suitable people who will be able to blend in to keep watch over her," Ashirah said, her lips curving into a smile.

"Good. Get it done. I'm going to go and visit Arkon," Zahir replied. The sooner he knew more about the girl and her allegiances, the better.

Zahir knew he was acting like he would if he found out he had a new enemy. He wanted to tear into Ezra's life and figure out whether or not she would be a threat.

Ezra didn't seem like an enemy, merely a girl in over her head. He couldn't trust that facade because his magic had been feeling off since she had been on the boat. He had been begging the Universe to give him a spark to ignite his fire again and instead had been sent an inferno.

* * *

THE PALACE WAS a decent walk from the Wands District, and Zahir made sure he was as incognito as possible. He could have vanished or teleported himself to San Marco, but he needed the time and the walk to think and use his physical body. When he took away the bright clothes, he was just another man on the street, and he liked it that way.

Zahir walked and thought. Golems could be helpful in the war effort, especially if Arkon's theory about the Varangians having other mages in their employ was true.

Using unstoppable clay warriors seemed ungentlemanly. The golems paled in comparison to the Cabal's plans to trap djinn.

Tightness squeezed his chest, and he quickly stared at the too blue sky above him. He had been trapped in jars before, knew the horrible, lonely darkness of it. He would do everything he could to stop it from happening again.

Zahir would give Ezra time to find out who the Cabal members were, and he'd take the information to Gio. He didn't want the djinn to take their revenge on humans because it would cause a whole world of drama for him.

At the palace, the guards recognized him immediately and didn't bother to stop him. Zahir stretched out his magic and tried to locate the Grand Sorcerer. His rooms had a habit of changing location due to Arkon's intense desire to be left alone.

Zahir felt the pathway that led to the current location and quickly moved along it before the magic changed on him. Arkon hadn't taken to setting booby traps yet, but Zahir knew he wanted to. He knocked on the door, and after receiving no answer, he pushed through Arkon's complex wards and walked in.

As usual, the sorcerer's apartment was a royal mess. Arkon lay on the couch facing his wall of Wolf Mage pictures. Every few moments, a small fireball appeared in his hand, and he threw it at one of the portraits.

"Ah, the busy life of the Grand Sorcerer," Zahir chuckled.

"Go away. I'm too hung over to spar with you," Arkon groaned and rolled onto his side.

Zahir walked carefully through the scattering of spell designs on the floor and placed a hand on Arkon's shoulder.

"Come on, sorcerer. I'll take you for some air and food and a djinn hangover cure you won't ever forget," Zahir coaxed him.

There was a long pause before the sorcerer mumbled, "Can I have the cure first?"

"Go and clean yourself up." Zahir poked him until he sat up.

Arkon stood up and stretched. "Fine. Wait here. Don't touch anything."

"I wouldn't dream of it," Zahir replied with a grin. Arkon scowled and disappeared towards the bathroom.

Zahir wasn't a snoop, even when he was tempted, so he sat on the vacated couch. He amused himself by repairing all the damaged posters of the Wolf Mage and the abused wall behind it. If the propaganda posters were to be believed, she was a living saint. Zahir had met saints before and highly doubted it. Using divine power would make her a cleric at most.

Still, there was something unnerving about the silvery Nordic hair and piercing gray eyes. She was beautiful and talented and dangerous.

Zahir was sure her game with Arkon would only end with one of them dead. If the war ended tomorrow, he had no doubt the sorcerer would track her down. Obsession didn't fade until it was satiated.

You should heed your own advice, his consciousness pricked him. Zahir refused to believe he had reached the point of obsession with Ezra. It was merely a curiosity. He didn't understand her power, and for the most part, he ignored magical abilities in humans. He needed his expert.

Arkon emerged from the bathroom a different man. He had

showered and was dressed in clean clothes. Zahir got up and fixed the buttons on his waistcoat.

"Help. My head is killing me," Arkon complained.

Zahir's magic thrummed, and he sketched a symbol on Arkon's forehead. The sorcerer groaned as the magic hit him.

"There we are, *habibi*. I'll make it all better," Zahir crooned at him.

Arkon sighed as the magic cleared the pain away. "If you teach me how to do that, I will call you Daddy forever."

Zahir pinched his chin. "That's Baba to you."

"Feed me, Baba, and tell me I'm pretty," Arkon said, batting his long lashes at him.

"Come along then, my dear sorcerer. I need you focused," Zahir replied, opening the door for him.

"Good luck with that," Arkon said but followed him anyway.

CHAPTER NINE

*a*rkon cast a glamor over them as soon as they walked out of the palace. Zahir tutted at him, but Arkon only shrugged.

"If I don't do it, people always stop me because they want something," Arkon grumbled. "My plate is full of dealing with Gio. He's being a tyrant."

Zahir shook his head. "My dear boy, I have served tyrants before, and trust me, Gio is not one of them. He wants the war to end; that's all."

"I am but one man," Arkon argued.

"You are more than that. If you are feeling the pressure, let another magician step up and take over the responsibility of the Wolf Mage. This is a democracy, after all. Retire."

"Absolutely not. She's mine to deal with. It's this other magic user that's impersonating her that I don't like," Arkon replied.

Zahir led them to a restaurant next to the Ponte dei Dai and was instantly greeted by the owner with a kiss on the cheek and taken to a private area in the back, away from the other patrons.

"You've never taken me here before," Arkon said, staring about.

"I thought we would both appreciate the privacy today."

Arkon nibbled on some bread. "Spit it out then. I know you want something."

"Me? I couldn't just want your company?"

"Flattered, but I know better. You're bothered about something."

Zahir waited until their wine had been delivered and they both had a glass. "I had an unusual petitioner barge her way onto my ship a few days ago. The little sparrow sung me an interesting tale, and I need to know if she's working for you."

Arkon frowned. "What's her name?"

"Ezra Eliyahu. Lives in the Ghetto Nuovo."

"Not a Raven. What song was she singing to get you so worked up?"

Zahir ended up telling Arkon the whole problem without stopping for input. Arkon was one of the few people he trusted to keep it a secret. The sorcerer lived off them and knew better than to divulge any that could put him on Zahir's bad side. They had ended up as each other's confessors in a way, and they both needed it.

"Golems. Fuck, that's all we need," Arkon said when Zahir was done.

"They don't bother me as much as a girl who has the abilities to bring them to life," Zahir replied.

Arkon rubbed his stubbled chin. "I would have to see her use the power myself. Sigil work is as common as dishwater."

"Sigil work drawn in the air without tools and only an intention. Because that's what it looked like."

Arkon hummed. "That is the strange part. Sigils are usually drawn out to cement your intention. I burn my spells in order to give them an extra burst of energy to get them to act faster. From what you're telling me, her magic is instantaneous?"

"Yes, she literally did this—" Zahir wiggled a finger at him. "And Asim and the others were high as kites. She ripped through my wards like they were paper. I'd be insulted if I wasn't also impressed."

Arkon's grin was crooked. "Takes a lot to impress you. Is she pretty?"

"Some would think so," Zahir said, not biting at that bait. "I thought we were done with conspiracies for a while. Djinn hating magicians are bad for business, and all they do is piss me off."

"You trust this girl to find them?"

"I know what it's like to be captured against your will. It motivates you in a way you can't imagine."

Arkon frowned. "Binding someone like that is a hanging offence on its own. We need to find out if they've used it on others. There's something else I don't understand."

"What's that?" Zahir asked, filling his glass.

"The three nights in the deal. What's up with that? It's not like you to add that kind of clause."

Zahir shifted, unable to bullshit Arkon. The sorcerer always knew when he was lying. It was incredibly inconvenient. "I don't really know. Perhaps I wanted to prove that not all djinn are bad?"

"And how are you going to do that exactly? Really, I'm curious because she was clearly raised with at least one prejudiced parent, and I don't think even you are capable of seducing someone with that kind of mistrust built into her."

"I'm very clever and handsome. I'm sure I'll figure something out."

Arkon's mouth twitched. "I thought you said she wasn't pretty."

"I said some would think she is. She's interesting. It goes a lot further than pretty," Zahir argued.

"I agree with you there. If she's as good with magic as you say, maybe I should meet her. Assess the pretty situation for myself," Arkon said, eyes innocent.

"You will stay away from her until I say so. This is a Wands problem to solve."

Arkon raised his hands. "I thought the purpose of telling me this was because you wanted my help."

"I wanted to know if you had a claim on her. You don't, which means she's mine."

Arkon bit the inside of his cheek, trying to hold in his laughter. "I've never seen you be this ridiculous over someone. You don't even know her."

"But I want to. That's a change. I like mysteries, and I haven't had a decent one in decades."

"You talking about the girl or the golem-making Cabal?"

"Both. No one has been ambitious enough to go up against the djinn."

"Just don't vaporize them when you find them. If they are a part of the Jewish Quarter, they are Gio's problem, not yours."

Zahir huffed in frustration. "I haven't forgotten, sorcerer. I will find out who they are and hand them over."

"And then what? Because Ezra knows how to influence djinn, and if she gets pissed off at you or any of the others, she could cause massive problems."

Zahir smiled. "That's why I need to win her to our side."

"And if you don't?"

"Then I will kill her, and that will be that."

Arkon sighed. "You are one scary bastard when you want to be."

"Takes one to know one, sorcerer." They shared a smile. "I won't do it unless I have to. She's unique, like Dom's Stella, and there aren't too many rare things left in the world anymore."

Arkon looked thoughtful. "Maybe I could get Stella to look into this a little for us."

"I'm sure your newest apprentice and Raven would be up for the challenge, but I don't know if risking her is a good idea. Domenico will not take it well if anything should happen to her," Zahir warned him. The shedu prince of Venice was over-protective when it came to his lovely mate despite the lightning magic she wielded.

"Very well, but keep her in mind. Women have a way of getting through to other women, and I have a feeling you're going to need all the help you can get with this one," Arkon replied.

"Oh, please. I have been seducing since before your kind were a twinkle in the Creator's eye," Zahir huffed in reply. "You will make some inquiries with your contacts about this Cabal of the Wise?"

"Of course I will. Secret societies are never as secret as they think they are. I'll even do the courtesy of keeping Ezra out of it," Arkon said. Because he couldn't help being a bastard, he added, "For now, anyway."

"Don't make threats, *habibi*. I like you too much to swat you like a bug."

Arkon laughed with evil glee. "Someone has a crush. What's your plan of attack?"

"There's no plan. I'm going to get comfortable and wait for her to come to me," Zahir replied.

"I hope you have a good book ready to go. Something tells me you'll be waiting a while."

Zahir hated it when Arkon was right.

CHAPTER TEN

*E*zra woke the following day to her arms burning. She screamed into wakefulness when she realized she wasn't dreaming.

"Stop!" she begged. Her vision cleared, and she saw the two men standing over her. She had fallen asleep on the couch in Judah's study the night before, her mind still working on the puzzles he had left her.

"Stop, please, stop. I'm awake!" she screamed. The pain in her arms stopped, and she fought not to vomit. "What is wrong with you people? You couldn't just wake me up like a normal person?"

"You can't ignore this like you did when we knocked on the door," the man said. It was the same one from the other night with the intense eyebrows. A young man was standing next to him and hadn't stopped staring at her. Ezra sat up and rubbed at her tender arms. It was then she realized it wasn't a man at all; it was a golem.

"I thought you said my father didn't help you," she said, getting up to inspect the golem. In the low light, it could easily be mistaken for a man.

"Judah didn't make him. I did," a new voice said. Another man came into the office with a steaming cup of coffee. He had black hair, dark eyes, and looked rumpled around the edges. Maybe she wasn't the only one who had a rude wake-up call that morning.

"By all means, help yourself," Ezra snapped.

"I made extra for you. Wow, the famous Ezra. Judah would never shut up about you," he said.

Ezra ignored that jab and went back to the golem. "Beautiful work. Are you an artist?"

"Amongst other things," he replied.

Ezra held a hand over the golem's face and felt familiar magic. "Judah made this *shem* for you? I thought it didn't work."

"It works, but not for very long," Mr. Intense Eyebrows said. "I brought it here in case you can see something we have missed."

Probably a lot of things, knowing Judah. Her father clearly had a plan to fuck with the Cabal, and Ezra wanted to uphold that family tradition.

"Maybe it's not the *shem* at all, but the clay," she said, looking at Mr. Artist.

He narrowed his eyes. "There is nothing wrong with my clay. It was made to the very instruction."

"Judah's instructions?" Ezra asked, raising a dark brow. So much for them being the Cabal of the Wise. "Seems to me that there might be nothing wrong with the *shem* after all."

"Is there a way for you to test it?"

Ezra touched the golem's hand, admiring the craftsmanship despite her annoyance. "The clay or the *shem*?"

"Both," the older man replied. "You are right. We have no idea if the clay is the problem."

"I can find out," Ezra said.

His expression darkened. "Show me right now."

Ezra's arms burned in warning. Fuck this guy. "I need the *shem*. And that coffee."

Mr. Artist's eyes narrowed. "Get your own."

"Shut up and give it to her," the man snapped. The younger man let out a huff and shoved the cup toward her. Ezra smiled and took it, having a big mouthful. It was too bitter, but the look of annoyance on his face made it taste sweeter.

The room sizzled with magic, and Ezra turned as the golem opened its mouth. Mr. Intense Eyebrows took the scroll from its mouth and gave it to her. She didn't have to unroll it to know that the sigil on it was different from the one Judah and she had made together. She needed to give them something so they would leave her alone for a few more days.

"Follow me," she said, taking the scroll and the coffee and heading for the basement.

When Judah and Ezra had created their golem, they had destroyed their *shem* only hours after getting it to work. Like most of the magic she created, the sigil had stayed in Ezra's mind in perfect recall. She could make it right there and then if she wanted to.

Ezra had wanted to destroy the golem too, but Judah wouldn't have it. They had made it together and wanted to remember the time they spent working on it. She turned on the lamps because the basement hadn't been fitted with the crystal lanterns.

The basement had gotten even more cluttered since she had been in it last. There was no hiding the tall wooden box leaning against the brick wall like a coffin.

"What are we doing down here?" Mr. Artist said.

"Checking your work," Ezra replied. She pulled the lid off the box and revealed the golem inside. Her heart hurt looking at its fine glazed features. She pressed two fingers over the clay man's lips, and he opened his mouth.

"I wondered what happened to Judah's golem. He said it was

destroyed," Mr. Intense Brows commented. "It is beautiful work."

"Thanks," Ezra said grudgingly. She placed the *shem* inside of its mouth, and the golem shuddered to life.

"Mistress," the golem said in a deep scratchy voice.

"Come out of there and let us look at you," Ezra instructed. The golem did as it was told.

"So it was the clay that was defective? I swear, Zachariah, I copied Judah's instructions to the letter," the artist said.

"I know you did. Judah was playing with you guys, and you didn't realize." Ezra chuckled, making note of the man's slip of his boss's name. *Idiot.* She brushed some straw off the golem's shoulders. "How about you take this one with you and see how the *shem* holds up in a proper golem?"

Zachariah moved in front of the golem. "It might pass as human if you have a coat and a hat to hide the shine on him."

"No problem," Ezra said. She went through the boxes that were meant to be donated before she left and found one of Judah's coats and a squashed fedora that she was getting rid of. She dressed the golem and commanded it to obey Zachariah.

"You are being very helpful. Too helpful," Mr. Artist said.

"I never said I was your enemy. Besides, I'm bound to help, and I want my freedom. What do I care why you guys want golems? It's not my business," she said with a shrug.

"You are far more pragmatic than Judah. We could do great things together," Zachariah told her. He touched her cheek gently. "Be good, and we will be friends in no time."

"Sure we will," she replied, wanting to break his finger and scrub her face with salt.

They all went back upstairs, the golem following them dutifully. It hurt to see it walk out of her house, but Ezra didn't have a choice. They should have destroyed it and not been sentimental.

"Keep working on Judah's spells. We will know soon enough if this golem works better than the last," Zachariah said.

"No problem. Maybe don't wake me up with torture next time. I'm a reasonable person. I don't need the extra motivation," Ezra replied and forced a smile onto her face.

"Perhaps. We will be keeping a close eye on you all the same," he said, and the three of them disappeared across the square.

"Fuck you both," Ezra whispered. She waited a few moments to ensure they were gone before locking the door. She raced back to Judah's study and dug about on the top of the bookshelf. She pulled down the recording device she had hidden up there the night before. Judah had been right to keep his office monitored.

"Please work, please work," she whispered. She turned on the artifice, and it hummed to life. Images of the two men and Ezra screaming hovered in the air in front of her. "Got you bastards."

Ezra chewed her lip. Surely, Zahir would have a way to track the men down with images alone. She couldn't risk going to the djinn again, not if Zachariah had people watching her house. She grinned. He wasn't the only one. She had felt djinn magic after her visit to the king. Maybe he was watching her too.

Ezra took the crystal out of the machine, slipped it into her pocket, and grabbed her purse. She walked out into the sunshine and went to check the market that had been set up in the square.

Ezra bought fruit and bread, browsing through the stalls until she felt a flicker of djinn magic. A woman was selling handmade jewelry.

"What pretty necklaces," Ezra said and gave the woman a smile. "I don't suppose you could get a message to your king for me?"

The woman's smile slipped. She looked so human that Ezra would have never picked her for a djinn except for the magic. "I have no king, *signorina*."

"It's okay, I know Zahir sent you. Tell him I need to see him, but I'm being watched. I have information he wants," Ezra said.

The woman's eyes flashed with gold. "You had better. He's not a patient creature. You see the old man playing chess over there? That's the other spy," she said with a smile. Another customer came to the stall, and the djinn wrapped a necklace and passed it to Ezra. "An excellent choice, *signorina*. I hope it brings you luck. As for your other inquiry, I will see if my craftsman is free to meet with you to discuss a commission."

"Thanks. It's a time sensitive project," Ezra replied and walked home. She let her eyes slide over the men playing chess in the sunshine. There was no magic coming off them at all.

It was late afternoon when a phoenix unexpectedly flew through the window of the study. It opened its mouth, letting out a cry before it exploded on the carpet.

"Ahh! Don't set my house on fire!" Ezra scrambled to pat out the flames that were scattered over the papers she had been working on.

Fiery words appeared in the air. It was an address on the other side of Cannaregio with the words, "PARTY. TONIGHT. Z."

"Finally," Ezra murmured and went to get ready to meet with the King of the Djinn.

CHAPTER ELEVEN

*E*zra didn't know what to expect from a djinn party, so she wore what she usually would for work. Leather pants and a dark red silk top that matched the hidden streaks of scarlet in her hair. She wore it up because the night was humid, fixing her heavy curls into place with two silver clips. Dark-rimmed eyes and a slash of burgundy lipstick finished off the look. She wasn't there to impress anyone; she just needed to blend into a crowd, get Zahir the crystal, and get out again.

"You can do this. It's a party like any other," she told her reflection.

Outside, the night was warm with the scents of the sea and people cooking. The men who had been watching the house were gone, but Ezra didn't think that she was alone. She hurried through the square and into the narrow streets.

Ezra heard the party long before she reached it. It was on the edges of the district where Wands met with Swords. The house was lit up on the inside, music pounding hard through the walls. Two men were guarding the front door where a line of people formed.

Ezra let her magic trickle out and confirmed that both of

the guards were human and not djinn. In fact, she couldn't see one djinn at all. She double checked the address she had scrawled on a piece of paper to make sure she was in the right place.

A guard spotted her and gestured her to come forward. Frowning, Ezra moved from the line and up to him.

"Boss said to let you in straight away. He said you will find him on the second floor," he said and opened the wooden door for her.

"Okay? Thanks," she replied and hurried into the dimly lit hallway.

The music pounded, the walls vibrating with an Arabic pop. The air above her was stained with metallic colors, and she wondered what the hell they were smoking. She could feel the djinn hidden amongst the party goers, their magic sending a buzz through the air that was intoxicating all on its own.

A large black djinn appeared in front of her. "Ah, the pretty girl from the boat has come to party with us," he said in his deep bass voice. "I am Asim."

"Ezra," she said with a smile. "I'm sorry about making you all high, but it was an emergency."

"Not to worry, butterfly," he replied and laughed brightly. He conjured a bright pink cocktail. "For you, lovely. Don't worry, it's only alcohol and magic. You are a favorite of the king, and no human or djinn will harm you in this place."

"Thank you." Ezra drank some of the cocktail, and raspberries burst onto her tongue. It made her feel like they were laughing all the way down her throat. "I don't suppose you know where the king is? He asked me to meet him."

"Just follow the magic, butterfly," Asim said and disappeared with a laugh.

Ezra pressed her way through groups of people, searching the dim lights for Zahir before giving up and letting her magic search for him like Asim suggested. A vortex of restrained, burning power pulsed back to her, making her magic tingle as it brushed playfully against her.

Ezra followed the sensation until she found a crammed dance floor. She couldn't see Zahir. Her body began moving to the beat of its own accord.

When you can do nothing else, you dance. Ezra gave herself over to it, swaying her way into the crowd before letting the music drown her senses. She registered the spicy desert scent before an arm came around her waist.

"Fancy meeting you here," Zahir's deep voice purred in her ear. "Are you having a good time?"

"I couldn't find you, so I thought I'd blend in and let you find me," Ezra said, her heart rate picking up its pace. She didn't move his hand away.

"And now I have. This is a familiar scene to you with all your Florence work?" he asked.

Ezra kept swaying. "Why? You want to hire me?"

"I might. Show me what you can do, little sparrow." The King of the Djinn wasn't asking. His hair was mussed, and eyeliner was smudged around his eyes in a way that made him appear more casual and less intimidating than she had last seen him. It made her feel bolder than what was good for her. Ezra turned slowly in his embrace and put her arm around his neck. His hands dropped to her hips, his dark eyes flashing with magic.

"Watch so you don't miss it," Ezra said. She couldn't resist the urge to show off a little. She held up a finger, and her magic traced a glowing golden sigil in the air. It wasn't necessary to reveal the shape of it, but there was something dangerous about Zahir that made her want to impress him. She gave the hovering sigil a little flick, sending it up to the ceiling before it exploded in a rain of tiny glowing stars. The crowd went crazy, trying to catch them like snowflakes. Wherever they hit, a little buzz went through them, djinn and human alike.

Ezra laughed at Zahir's dazzled expression. He was staring at her in a way that made heat bloom in her stomach.

Little stars were glowing in their hair before one landed on her mouth. Zahir lifted her chin to look at it.

"Incredible," he said.

Ezra's breath caught as he bent his head and licked the star off her bottom lip. Heat and magic burned through her, blowing out her pupils with the rush of it.

Zahir hummed and tugged her closer. "We need to get out of here without raising any suspicion, so play along, sparrow."

Ezra nodded, her brain incapable of forming words. Zahir smiled, placed both hands on her flushed cheeks, and kissed her. Ezra's hand went to his waist, drawing him closer to her as he tasted her lips in a slow exploration.

Her breathing was erratic. She knew that this was a terrible idea, but her body wasn't listening to her. She let the Djinn King hold her in an unbreakable grip and take whatever he wanted.

Ezra made a point of getting kissed often, but this kiss made her bones feel like they were melting. Her brain was flashing red lights at her. She ignored them and leaned into it. Zahir let out a low, husky sound before yanking her closer and deepening the kiss. It was rough and taking, and Ezra had never been kissed like it before. His magic was swamping her, his body so hard and warm pressing into her. His tongue slipped into her mouth, his piercing creating a strangely pleasant sensation. She tried not to think of what it would be like licking other parts of her body. Her hand was sliding into his shirt when he pulled back.

"We have to stop," Zahir said against her lips. His grip on her slowly loosened. "Walk with me."

"O-Okay?" she stammered, feeling shaky. She knew she would feel ridiculous later, but it had been too good of a kiss for her to care much.

Zahir took her hand and led her through the crowd. Ezra followed him, still a little dazed with her body thrumming.

"Are you okay, my king?" a djinn asked, his aqua eyes surveying Ezra.

"Never better. I'm stepping out to take care of something," Zahir said with a devilish laugh.

"Have fun." The djinn nodded and pushed open a panel in the wall.

Magic tingled against Ezra's skin as Zahir pulled her through the hidden door and into a corridor. She couldn't be sure, but she had the distinct feeling they were no longer in the same building.

"What is this place?" she asked.

"The back way," Zahir replied before opening another door. They stepped into a bedroom covered in richly woven carpets, colorful lamps, and the biggest bed Ezra had ever seen.

Zahir shut the door behind her, and the music disappeared altogether. Her ears were ringing at the sudden silence.

"Drink?" he asked and began to pour something from a decanter.

"Sure," Ezra said, her mind still trying to reconcile the magic that it would take to build pathways to other places. She tried very hard not to stare at the bed.

Zahir pressed a glass into her hand. "You wanted to see me?" He was suddenly a completely different man from the one who had kissed her on the dance floor.

It was an act, you idiot. You are forgetting who you are dealing with, she scolded herself.

Zahir sprawled out on a couch, looking like the bored king she had first met. Ezra drained her drink, which turned out to be brandy, and pulled the crystal out of her bra. She didn't trust it being anywhere else.

"I have managed to get a recording of two of the men in the Cabal," she passed him the crystal.

"Hmm, still warm," he said with a twinkle in his eyes. Okay, maybe not a totally different man from the one she had made out with. He held the crystal up to the light. "What's on it?"

"The man who put the manacles on me is on it. His lackey slipped and called him Zachariah. If you have the artifice, I can show you," Ezra replied, charging ahead. The kisses had left her confused and unsteady. She didn't like feeling either of those things. It was like the Djinn King was designed to throw her off her game.

"No need. I can do it," Zahir said. He squeezed the crystal, and his power flared. Ezra's screams echoed through the room as the projection came to life. She flinched and rubbed at her arms, trying not to relive the pain. Zahir's expression darkened as he watched Zachariah and the artist question her.

"What did you give them?" he asked, letting the power go, so the crystal blinked out.

"I put their *shem* into the golem I made with my father. I know it's faulty, but it bought me some time to get this to you. Do you know who these guys are?" Ezra asked.

"No, but I will find them," he growled. He got to his feet and took her hands, his fingers tracing over her skin. "Are you still hurt? You were screaming. I can take the pain away."

Ezra softened, feeling strangely touched. "I'm fine. It only hurts when the bonds are being interfered with. There's no lasting physical damage."

Zahir's frown deepened. "No, only psychological. Anything else?"

"I'm being watched and not only by you. I can't do anything about it, but maybe you have some friends that can follow them? They might lead you back to other Cabal members. I don't think I'll have time to identify them all. I need to figure out ways to look like I'm co-operating with them without helping them," Ezra said. Zahir still hung onto her forearms, and she didn't pull away.

"I'll look into it. Anything else?" he repeated, fingers gently moving down her skin.

"I have a name. I don't know who it is or if it will be much use. My father left me a message. He said the Cabal was planning to sell the golems to a Varangian man called Ingvar Hardrada. I've never heard of him."

"I have," Zahir hissed, his grip on her tightening. "If he is involved, we are in deeper shit than we both expected. This is getting too dangerous for you. I don't like it."

"I don't like it either, but I'm still your best shot at uncovering all of this," Ezra argued. She froze as Zahir stroked her cheek.

"I don't want them to kill you, sparrow. Your magic is too interesting, and we have a bargain," he said. He lifted her arm to where the three marks were tattooed. He held her gaze as he kissed the spot, his stubble scraping deliciously against her skin. "Stay with me tonight. I can keep you safe, and you can work off one of these marks."

Ezra's whole body screamed, 'Yes!' but her mouth said, "Thanks, but I have other plans, and I don't need protecting."

"What plans? With whom?" Zahir asked, eyes narrowing.

"Stuff. Plans. Work," Ezra stammered. "I need to be focussed, and all this has thrown out my concentration."

If Zahir kissed her again, she knew she would throw caution to the wind and stay. He didn't. He only let out a frustrated sigh and released her.

"I will find out who the men are. Try to stay safe, sparrow." Zahir walked over to a wall and opened another invisible panel. "This will open outside the house. Go straight home."

Ezra felt her devilish side rearing its ugly head. He had teased her with the kissing, and she was in a mood to tease back.

"Don't tell me what to do," she said haughtily.

Zahir's eyes flared. "Do as you're told, or I'll be using one of those marks to teach you some discipline."

She paused by the door and leaned in as if to kiss him. Zahir sucked in a surprised breath, but she didn't close the charged space between them.

"Don't threaten me with a good time, my king," she whispered, pulling away and stepping through the door before he could stop her.

CHAPTER TWELVE

*Z*ahir arrived at the Vianello Publishing House the following morning before it had opened its doors. The person who did open them took one look at the Djinn King in his bright indigo and gold robes and let out a cry of surprise before disappearing once more.

"What have I told you about scaring my staff?" a beautiful, blonde-haired woman demanded. Stella Aladoro was a fulmian mage, able to wield electricity and lightning, one of Arkon's spies, and the wife to the most powerful shedu in the whole of the Republic. She was also a talented artist and a smartass. Zahir liked her immensely.

"Apologies, my love, but I am in a mood, and I needed to see you at once," Zahir said. His mood involved a pretty sigil mage who had refused to let him pleasure her within an inch of her life.

Stella's green eyes narrowed as they studied him. Finally, she opened the door wider and gestured to him. "Come on, let's get you some coffee."

Zahir followed her through the publishing house and to the kitchen located at the back of it. Stella already had a full pot of coffee on the go, and she placed a plate of fresh pastries in front of him.

"Where is your *amore*?" Zahir asked and picked up a croissant.

Stella took out two prettily painted cups. "Dom had an early meeting with Gio this morning."

"You don't seem surprised to see me." Zahir accepted the steaming cup from her and had a sip.

Stella sat down opposite him with the plate of pastry in between them. "Arkon told me to expect you. He said that you might have need of my assistance. I didn't expect you so soon, but here you are."

"That sorcerer needs to mind his own goddamn business," Zahir huffed.

"So you don't need my help with a certain beautiful, talented, intriguing magician that you have become entangled with? Or has there been no entangling, which is why you are pouting?" Stella grinned, her delicate fingers pulling apart a cherry Danish and offered him some. She knew that the djinn shared food as a sign of trust. Zahir took it and had a bite. He did need advice. He just hated admitting it.

"She came to me last night with a crystal containing the images of these two men." Zahir reached into his robe and passed her photos that he had pulled from the projection. It showed both men standing over Ezra. He had watched it over and over, her cries of pain stuck in his brain like needles. He would do such terrible things to those men if he ever got his hands on them.

Stella took the pictures and studied the black-and-white images. "Do they have names?"

"The older one is called Zachariah. I don't know the other one, but he is an artist. A sculptor good enough to create a golem. How much did Arkon tell you?" Zahir asked. He knew whatever he told Stella would get back to Dom, but without

Zahir's permission, it wouldn't go further. They were good friends like that.

"He told me all of it. You know how he likes to gossip. To be honest, he was more intrigued about you having a crush on a girl than he was about golems being sold within the Republic." Stella tapped the picture. "Is that the lovely Ezra on the ground?"

"Yes, it is. She assured me that she was no longer in pain, but I want to tear these men apart for hurting her." Zahir took a long drink from his cup. He had slept badly, partly from the revelations Ezra had told him. Mostly, from wanting her and being rejected. He tried not to dwell on it. "She also found out that they were going to sell the golems to the Varangians. She had a name of one of the nobles that is in Arkadi's court. We need to find out who these men are. I hate conspiracies that aren't my own. They aren't nearly as fun."

Stella was frowning as she selected another pastry and had a big bite. "If the Varangian nobles are involved, this could be more dangerous than we originally thought. Are you sure you don't want to intervene? Ezra could get hurt."

"I know that. I offered to have her stay with me last night, and she turned me down. She is determined to see it through, no matter the danger."

Stella smirked. "She turned *you* down? Even though she owes you three nights? And you just let her walk away?"

"I never specified what we would be doing on those nights. I would never force a woman, even if a bargain was involved." Zahir sniffed irritably. "I made her the offer, and she said no. I was *rejected*, Stella. *Me*."

Stella started giggling. "Why are you surprised? I rejected you too. It's bound to happen occasionally. Maybe you're not her type."

"Bah! I am everyone's type, and I didn't make you a serious offer. I knew you were mates with Dom, and I was only doing it to piss him off," Zahir said. He stuffed more pity sugar into his mouth. "I was surprised Ezra said no, considering she kissed me only moments beforehand."

Stella's brows shot up in surprise. "Did she now? You seem to be really put out by this. You had best tell me the whole story."

Zahir hadn't needed advice about a woman for so many thousands of years that he couldn't remember the last time he went for help about it.

He found himself telling Stella of the party at the house, he and Ezra dancing, and finally kissing her. He could still taste Ezra's full lips and the beguiling flavor of her magic. He had never been aroused like that over a simple kiss. It was an all-encompassing, drowning feeling that he had thought he was incapable of having.

Stella listened patiently to him ranting, a small smile creeping over her face. "It sounds to me that you were hot, and then you were cold, and she got spooked. Not that I blame her. You do have quite the reputation for being a man whore. She is smart enough to resurrect old magic, so she's definitely too smart to fall for your tricks."

"I don't want to trick her! I want to get to know her, prefer-ably with no clothes on. I'm genuinely worried about her safety, and I don't know how to protect someone who wants to put herself in danger," Zahir complained. He got out of his chair and began to pace the kitchen. He had set guards to watch her house, but if Zachariah turned up again, he could hurt her, and they would be able to do nothing about it.

"How can I help?" Stella said, pouring him another cup. "You seem to genuinely like this girl. I can't imagine that happens very often even in a djinn's lifespan. I can be your middleman if you want to pass messages to her."

"And how would your husband feel about that? As you have pointed out, if the Varangians are involved, it's going to be dangerous. Especially when Ezra doesn't produce magic for the golems to work. They will retaliate, and I would hate for you to get caught in the crossfire. I would also hate to see what Dom would do to me."

"It's Raven business. He doesn't need to know everything. Just that I've made a new friend." Stella tapped her chin. "I can do a trip to that district today with a delivery. I am sure that a magician like her would appreciate a fine journal to record all of her researching in."

Zahir smiled as he warmed to the idea. "Perhaps put in some nice stationery so she could write me occasionally? You can put it on my account with anything else you think that she might like."

It had been so long since he had even considered courtship that he didn't know what the rules were anymore. Gifts always seemed a good way to win a woman over.

"Arkon and I have been experimenting with paper messaging, and I might have a good way for you to be able to communicate with her without worrying that your messages will be intercepted." Stella placed the empty cups in the sink before she looped her arm through Zahir's. "Come with me, my friend, and let's spend some of your money."

CHAPTER THIRTEEN

*E*zra had slept terribly all night long. She had tossed and turned, a hunger in her belly for something she couldn't have. Well, maybe she could, but only for three nights.

You are being ridiculous. Ezra didn't have time to fantasize about the King of the Djinn or the way he kissed her. It was hard not to. Zahir was made of fantasies, and that was before she knew of the tongue piercing. She tried not to regret saying no to him the night before. It was the right thing to do. It didn't matter that it wasn't only physical. She was a student of magical history. Zahir had been there. He *was* magical history. The stories he could tell her, the magic he could show her... Ezra clamped down that train of thought.

Her rebellious nature always got her into trouble. It had made her leave Venice, and because of it, Judah was dead. It was better to keep her growing fascination with Zahir firmly in her spank bank and not let it out. It would only end in heartache anyway. Zahir would only be interested in her for as long as she worked for him. As soon as Zachariah and his colleagues were stopped, he would no doubt forget all about Ezra. She was getting too old to risk playing those kinds of games. She wouldn't be someone who could share either. Zahir would have his harem, and she would end up resentful. No, it was better to let that sleeping dog lie.

It was lunchtime when Ezra woke again. She had seen the dawn and was feeling disorientated. She also registered that someone was banging on her front door.

"Who could that be?" Ezra grumbled and pulled on a kimono. Zachariah and the Cabal would just have charged in. She grabbed a pencil off a bookshelf and twisted her hair up into a knot.

Stumbling downstairs, Ezra opened the door just as the woman on the other side of it lifted her hand to knock again. She was blonde and pretty and vaguely familiar.

"Oh, good, you are home! I was beginning to worry when nobody was answering." The woman patted the brightly wrapped package she was carrying. "I have a delivery for you from Zahir Matani, along with a message. May I come in?"

Ezra scanned the square, making note of the men playing chess again and the woman selling jewelry. It would seem that they were being watched from all sides again. Did they ever sleep?

"Of course you can. I'm Ezra," she said and opened the door wider for her to come in.

"I'm Stella. It's so good to meet you in the flesh. I've had the most amusing morning with Zahir. I never thought I would see him so out of sorts over a woman. Good to know that he's capable of being flustered every now and again."

Ezra flushed at the mention of Zahir. She shut the door behind her and locked it. That was when she realized who she had let into her house.

"You aren't Stella Aladoro, are you?" she asked, her voice coming out in more of a panicked squeak.

"I am. How did you know?" Stella replied.

Ezra huffed out a laugh. "My flat mate in Florence is an

absolute sucker for gossip. He pointed your picture out in the paper when you married Domenico."

"I hated that article. My mother-in-law insisted on the wedding being listed in the society pages. That's what happens when you marry into Swords royalty, I suppose." Stella let out a self-conscious laugh. "Don't worry, Ezra. I am nowhere near royalty. I am as common as they come. I just happen to have special abilities that haven't been seen in the Republic for a while. We are the same in that way."

Stella obviously knew more about what was happening with Ezra than she had thought.

"I take it Zahir has told you all about the bargain we have," Ezra said. She put on the hot water kettle and looked around for some coffee. Stella placed the wrapped packages on the kitchen table and joined her at the counter.

"He did. I am here to help you. Starting with, I will make coffee and you can go and get some clothes on. Sound good?"

Ezra laughed. "I don't think you are giving me a choice. Are you?"

"No, I'm not. I think you need a friend, and I am here to be that friend."

"Why? Because Zahir told you to?" Ezra asked and crossed her arms. She didn't need the Djinn King setting her up on play dates.

Stella shook her head. "No. It is because I know what it's like to get caught up in a conspiracy involving the Varangians and people who want to sell out Venice to them. I am uniquely qualified to be your friend. Now go and get some clothes on, and we will have coffee and talk."

Ezra found herself nodding in agreement and heading back up to her bedroom. She wasn't awake enough to argue with someone as forthright as Stella Aladoro.

Once she had washed off the remainder of last night's makeup and dressed in clean clothes, Ezra went back downstairs to find her mysterious guest. Not that she didn't think that Zahir had sent her, but she absolutely didn't trust her. Ezra was a lot of things. Stupid wasn't one of them.

Stella was sitting at the kitchen table with steaming cups of coffee. She pushed the wrapped package toward Ezra. "For you."

"What's this?" Ezra asked.

Stella's green eyes twinkled. "Little presents from your not-so-secret admirer."

Ezra didn't know what to make of that, so she opened up the package. Inside was a beautiful journal covered with indigo leather and stamped with a design of a bird. *A sparrow.* Ezra ran her fingers over it, her cheeks burning.

There was also an expensive fountain pen and violet colored ink. They were both stamped with the Vianello Publishing House's logo.

"These are lovely. Thank you so much," Ezra said and flipped through the thick paper.

"Thank Zahir. He picked them out for you this morning. They have another unique feature." Stella took the journal and opened the first page where a sigil had been drawn in silver paint. "This is a new messaging book that I have been designing. Anything you write in it, Zahir can read in his own journal. He thought it would be a safer way for you two to talk to each other, rather than risk his spies by approaching them directly. Why don't you try it out?"

Ezra uncapped the fountain pen and turned to a fresh page. *Thank you for your gifts. I like Stella*, she wrote.

Stella read over her shoulder and said, "I like you too."

Ezra was drinking her coffee when dark red writing rose on the page underneath her script: **You're welcome. Don't believe anything bad she says about me.**

Stella snorted. "You should believe *everything* I say about him. Including that he was very mopey that you didn't spend last night with him."

Ezra choked on her coffee. "He told you about that?"

"I believe he was trying to ask for my advice about it. I don't think he's actually been rejected for a long time and was struggling with how to deal with it. Fucking amusing to watch. I didn't think he even knew how to be awkward." Stella went and sat down again. She gave Ezra an expectant look. "Now, I want to hear your side of the story."

"I bet you do, but I don't know if I trust you enough. You have just walked into my house. You are acting like we are best friends, but I don't even know you," Ezra said and shut the journal.

Instead of being offended, Stella tilted back her head and let out a cackle of delighted laughter. "I am too old to play around anymore. I have decided that we are going to be friends, and that's that. I think it's easier just to be direct about it as opposed to trying to convince you. I can help you navigate this world that you are now stuck in."

"No offense, but a socialite princess can't help me with much."

Stella's eyes flashed with tiny bolts of lightning. "Oh, honey, I'm not a socialite princess. I'm a Raven."

Ice cold terror dumped down Ezra's spine. The Ravens were the secret network of spies that reported to the Grand Sorcerer himself. They never revealed their identity to anyone unless they were about to kill or arrest them.

"A Raven!" Ezra managed to squeak out. She was so fucking fucked.

"Take a breath. You're not in trouble with us," Stella reassured her. And then she told Ezra a wild story about forbidden magic, an even more forbidden romance, human trafficking, and dealing with those brave and stupid enough to try to make deals with the Varangians.

"So, you see, I've been in your shoes, and that's why I know you need someone you can trust," Stella finished. She tapped the journal. "You can trust him too. I know he acts like a brainless flirt, but he's one of the smartest, deadliest creatures in all the Republic."

"I've never seen him act like a brainless flirt, so I'll have to take your word on it," Ezra said, her mind spinning.

Stella waggled her eyebrows. "That's because he actually likes you. It's hilarious for me to watch, I can tell you."

"I don't think he likes me. He just wants to know who's behind the Cabal, and I'm the tool who will get it for him." Ezra decided she didn't have anything more to lose, so she stuck out her hand. "Ezra Eliyahu, it's nice to meet you."

Stella gave it a solid shake. "You too. I'm fascinated by your magic, but I really must know something. Why did you turn Zahir down? I mean… He's *Zahir*. The walking personification of sex. Do you like girls better? Is it because he never stops talking? I need to know."

Ezra blushed. "I had things to do, that's all."

"Things more important than possibly the best sex of your life?" Stella asked, her smile widening. "Because he's had thousands of years to figure out where the clit is."

Ezra burst out laughing. She really did like Stella. "He was acting weird, and it didn't feel like the right moment. He kissed me, then acted like the cold, bored king once we were alone, and then randomly asked me to sleep with him? I didn't think he was thinking clearly, and my day had been long enough."

Stella shook her head. "I knew he wasn't telling the story right. If it makes you feel better, he really isn't thinking clearly. He likes you, and not just because he sees you as a potential bed mate. It's left him all out of sorts and off his game. Do you like him?"

"I don't know him. I generally get to know someone before I sleep with them."

Stella leaned over and touched the marks on Ezra's arm.

"How do you feel about those? You must've felt something to agree to spending three nights with him."

"Scared and desperate is what I was feeling. He never specified what we would be doing with those three nights," Ezra argued.

"He said the same thing," Stella replied, the mischief back in her eyes. "I had a friend who once dated a djinn, and she said the sex was transcendental. That it was like a spiritual awakening level orgasm. That's got to make a girl curious, don't you think?"

Ezra let out a tight, awkward laugh before going into the cupboards and pulling out a bottle. "I can't have this conversation without wine."

"Now, we are talking." Stella grinned. "I knew befriending you was a good idea."

CHAPTER FOURTEEN

*A*fter Stella had left, Ezra spent the rest of the afternoon pleasantly buzzed while she worked her way through Judah's papers. She was contemplating a break when her new journal rustled its pages.

"Okay, that's not weird at all," she murmured and opened it up. Fresh red script streaked across the page: ***I'm in a meeting and very bored. Tell me how great you think I am.***

Who is this? Ezra wrote back, trying not to giggle. Seriously, the male djinn didn't lack for self-confidence.

Rude girl. I thought we were friends.

Your ego is big enough without me stroking it, Ezra replied honestly.

Would you like a list of other things you could stroke instead?

Ezra let out a burst of laughter. Zahir must've been bored to want to flirt with her. She tapped the pen on the desk before throwing caution to the wind.

I already have other things to stroke and can do it quite well on my own. She knew the conversation would go further into dangerous territory if she didn't change the subject. *Aren't you meant to be paying attention in council meetings?*

I'm sure I'm meant to do a lot of things. Nico is talking about the pirate's problem again, and it's hard to concentrate when a grown man is complaining this much.

*Nicolo D'Argento?! I wouldn't be able to concentrate either. That man is **fine.***

I suppose he is if you're into heroic and dashing.

Isn't everyone? Is he still single? Because I could use a date. Teasing Zahir was probably the most dangerous thing Ezra could do, but she couldn't help herself.

What are you working on? Zahir wrote back, clearly not biting the bait.

Ezra looked at the mess of sketches and notes before her. *Honestly? No idea. My father's stuff. He was never this chaotic. I shouldn't have left him alone.* Ezra wanted to scratch out the words as soon as she wrote them, but it was too late.

He was your parent, not the other way around. He made his choices, sparrow, Zahir replied.

Ezra sighed loudly to try to alleviate some of the pressure in her chest. He was right, but also wrong. Judah had become mentally and emotionally unmoored since Lucia's death. Ezra felt responsible for him because if she didn't look after him and keep him grounded, he wouldn't do it for himself.

I told myself the same thing when I left Venice. I knew better and went anyway. Now, he's dead, I'm enslaved, and if I don't figure out a way to trick the Cabal, we are all fucked, she scrawled back messily.

Your slavery is temporary, sparrow. I won't let them keep you. We have a deal, and I'm disinclined to share.

Ezra snorted. "That's not what I've heard, great king." She took a deep breath and wrote: *Go back to your meeting. I have work to do.*

She shut the book and tossed it to the other side of the study so she wouldn't be tempted to write to him again. It was a bad idea to get familiar in any way with Zahir. It would end badly, like every other relationship she had.

"You don't have a relationship. You have a bargain," she told herself angrily. She watched the crystal that her father had hidden again, trying to make notes of everything he said and showed. She paused on the image of the strange sigil.

"Now, you are a much better diversion," she said, and taking a fresh piece of paper from a stack, she began to draw. It wasn't until she finished the last curving line of it that she understood what she had drawn.

Sick, clawing dread scratched at her insides. "What did you do, Papa?" she whispered before resting her head on the desk and bursting into tears.

EZRA STARED up at the twinkling stars above her and had another mouthful from the wine bottle in her hand. She didn't know what time it was and didn't care. She was standing in her mother's small rooftop garden. Judah might have been terrible about looking after himself, but Lucia's garden was still pristine. He maintained it to honor her memory and feel close to her.

Ezra walked to the edge of the rooftop to look down at the square below. Her mind still felt sticky and gross from the magic of her father's sigil. Like all the magic she absorbed, it wasn't going anywhere. She would have to feel it for the rest of her life, unable to scratch it out even if she wanted to.

Ezra stared down at the people in the square below, going to the restaurant and walking arm in arm together. She swayed forward, and a hand grabbed out to stop her.

"Get back from that edge before you fly off it, sparrow," Zahir said, his grip on her unbreakable.

Ezra turned wonkily. "I wasn't going to jump."

"I'm more concerned with you toppling off accidentally in

your current state." Zahir pulled her gently away from the edge and back amongst the potted lemon and orange trees.

Ezra's drunken daze cleared a little. "What... What are you doing here?"

"I was concerned when you didn't write back to me," he replied. He looked about before snapping his fingers. Carpets and cushions rolled out in a space amongst the greenery. "Sit down before you fall, sparrow."

Ezra flopped backward on the mound of cushions. "Ohhh, softy soft." She looked around at the plants surrounding them. She pouted. "I loved Mamma's sunflowers. They are my favorite, and there're none."

Zahir stared down at her and folded his arms. He was wearing loose silk black pants and a dark green shirt that showed off his bronze arms and a delicious V of skin on his chest. Ezra's scattered thoughts went hazy. *Yum.*

"We can get you sunflowers later, sparrow. What happened? Why are you so drunk?" he asked, making her focus.

"Maybe I wanted to be. The party king can't judge me for drinking too much wine," she grumbled and pulled a cushion over her face. She didn't want to look at his handsome, glowering mug. Or do something dumb like tell him just how much she wanted to lick his face.

Zahir lay down on his side beside her and pulled the cushion away. "Talk to me, Ezra," he said softly. He never called her by her real name, and it made her feel all squishy in her guts.

She turned her head so she could look into his beautiful eyes. He really was unnaturally stunning. She wanted to suck on the emerald studs glinting in his ears.

"If you promise not to kill me, I'll tell you," she whispered. She thought of the magic, and her eyes welled with tears against her will.

Zahir brushed a thumb over her cheek, wiping one away. "I

already promised I wouldn't kill you. You know I won't. I can't. It's a part of the bargain."

Ezra stared up at the stars again so she wouldn't cry harder. She cleared her throat. "I went through the recording my father left for me. On it was…this glowing sigil. I thought it might be some special present just for me. A message that only I could read."

"And what was it, really?" Zahir's hand lifted to stroke her hair. It was a comforting gesture that made her want to cry more.

"It was the sigil to not only entrap a djinn, but to enslave them. It wasn't bound to any magic infused clay. They could put it on a pendent or a ring, anything they wanted." Ezra pressed her fists into her temples. "It's so awful, Zahir, and I don't know if he gave it to the Cabal. Not only that, but it's now also carved on the inside of my skull. I can't get it out. It will be there forever."

Tears slipped down her cheeks. The pain of the magic and the knowledge that Judah had actually created something so evil… It was too much.

"Don't cry, *habibi*. It's not your fault. None of this is your fault," Zahir said and put an arm around her, pulling her close.

"I'm so mad at him. How could he do such a thing?" Ezra was sobering up, and it was making her feel *everything*.

"You know how this Cabal operates. You don't know what they held over your father to force him to create such a thing. I don't blame you. I don't even blame him."

"Why not?"

"Because if I was forced to guess, I'd say they threatened your safety to get him to co-operate. I can't blame a father for trying to protect his daughter."

Ezra leaned back a little. "Even if it's going to hurt your people?"

"I have to think logically about this, not emotionally," Zahir said, his eyes going distant. "If the Cabal already had access to this sigil, why haven't they made a move to entrap any djinn? What's holding them back?"

Ezra scrubbed at the tears on her face. "I don't know. Perhaps because Judah tricked them about the golems, they are hesitant to entrap a djinn with a faulty sigil?"

"It's a good theory. I suppose we will just have to wait to find out," Zahir grinned, and Ezra's brain stopped working. "You would rescue me if I got trapped in a jar, wouldn't you?"

"All depends. How many wishes will you grant me?" Ezra asked. Zahir poked her, and she squirmed.

"Rude girl," he chided.

Ezra sat up and pushed her wild curls from her face. "If I'm so rude, what are you doing here?"

"Maybe I enjoy your rudeness. Everyone else is too scared to talk back to me or argue with me," Zahir said, resting on his elbows.

Ezra frowned. "That sounds kind of..."

"Boring? Yes, it is."

"No, I was going to say lonely," she replied.

Zahir's smile slipped a little. "Yes, I suppose it can be. I do love an argument too. You don't seem to be afraid of me at all, and maybe I find that refreshing."

"I'm afraid. I just don't show it. Your ego is big enough," Ezra replied.

"It's not the only thing," he teased. Ezra made the mistake of letting her eyes wander over his long body. He caught her watching, and his grin returned. Shit.

"Thanks for checking in on me. I'm sure you're busy doing king stuff," Ezra said, fidgeting slightly. If he kept looking at her with that smile, she was going to do something stupid.

"My night is free, and I'm enjoying your company. Unless... You want me to leave?" Zahir asked and tucked a hand behind his head. Ezra's mouth watered.

"No?" Ezra said when she really should have said the opposite. She liked his company too and couldn't deny it anymore. She lay back down on her side to face him. "Tell me about your day. I need something to keep my mind away from wanting to summon my father's shade so I can yell at it."

Zahir lifted a brow. "You really want to know?"

"Yeah, I really do," Ezra said and settled in.

CHAPTER FIFTEEN

*Z*ahir found himself in the strangest circumstance. He was actually telling someone about his day, the frustrations of being in charge of the Wands District and how the Wolf Mage continued to vex Arkon.

Zahir realized that he didn't really have unnecessary conversations with people anymore. They were either giving him information or he was passing on orders. It was strangely refreshing to just talk to someone. Especially when that someone was the woman he couldn't stop thinking about, no matter how much he tried.

Mid-conversation, Zahir had produced some alcohol-free cocktails. Ezra was sober again, but she wasn't less open or interesting. He found her mind and wit sharp and scathing, and he liked it immensely.

"So how old are you anyway?" she asked, propping her head up with a hand.

Zahir thought about it. "Old enough to remember what Solomon's temple was like when it was freshly built and when your people would dance with the djinn long into the night. You didn't hate us then, and the world seemed so full of wonder."

"My father had a saying, '*When you can do nothing else, you dance.*' In retrospect, it was one of the wisest things he said to me," Ezra replied.

Zahir smiled. "Wise indeed. What else did he tell you?"

She gave him a cryptic smile. "To stay away from the djinn and to never speak your name in case you hear me."

"You're serious?" Zahir tilted his head back and laughed. "I'm too old to care what people say about me. I suppose it would depend on *how* you said my name, as to whether I paid any attention. If it was a kind of breathless little moan, I might be more interested."

Ezra shook her head in despair. "You are incorrigible. Do you ever stop flirting?"

"I can't help it. I want to kiss you, and it's very distracting."

"You want to kiss me?" Ezra said, frowning like she didn't believe him.

Zahir nodded. "Badly."

"Huh. What's holding you back?" she asked, tilting her head curiously.

"Last time I did, you shut me down. Despite the rumors, I don't have a harem with a revolving door, and I don't go where I'm not wanted," Zahir replied. He was being honest, a rare thing when he was interested in bedding someone. Ezra deserved better than deception. He genuinely liked her. It was going to be problematic in the future, and he still couldn't stop.

"It's not that you weren't wanted," Ezra mumbled so softly, he almost missed it.

Zahir grinned. "What was that?"

"Nothing."

"The hell it was. Stop pretending you don't like me. It's very annoying, and it's starting to hurt my feelings," Zahir huffed. She threw a cushion at him, and it bounced off his face.

"The disresp—" he began when she threw another. He grabbed it out of the air, tossed it over the side of the building, and pounced on her. Ezra let out a giggling squeak of surprise before Zahir kissed her like it was his last night on earth. Ezra melted underneath him, one leg curling around his and drawing him closer.

Thank the Creator. He slid his tongue along her lips, and she opened for him. Zahir had been craving her taste, the mysterious myrrh scent of her, the hot hiss of her power against his. He had stopped wondering what it was about her that drew him in. It didn't matter. Only having her mouth on him did.

Ezra moaned softly, and he flicked his pierced tongue into her mouth, stroking her own tongue languidly. Her hands threaded into his dark hair, giving it a gentle tug that had him hardening.

It's just kissing. Don't scare her, he tried to tell himself.

Ezra pulled back and blurted, "I'm not fucking you on the rooftop."

"Did I ask to fuck you, little sparrow?" he said, raising a brow.

"Isn't this... Aren't you here because of these?" Ezra asked, lifting her arm where her marks were.

"No. I'm here because I want to be." Zahir shook his head, and then a horrible thought occurred to him. "You're not kissing me because you feel obligated to because of them, are you?"

"No! God, no. I was enjoying the moment. I didn't know if you felt the same," she said. She covered her eyes with her hand. "Fuck, I've just ruined it, haven't I?"

Zahir moved her hand away and kissed it. "Not at all. You're right to question my motives. I would remove that part of the bargain if I could, but it's impossible now. It's not an obligation to have sex with me either. I wanted those nights to spend time with you to convince you that djinn aren't terrible. You have the power to control us if you wanted to. I wanted to try to...win you over, I suppose."

Ezra placed her hand on his chest, and his heart skipped. "I'd never hurt any of you. I can't help having this magic in my head, but I would never use it."

"I know." Zahir stroked her cheek, delighting in its velvety softness. "But just so we are clear, if you want to have sex, you wouldn't regret it."

Ezra laughed, and her cheeks turned pink. "Is that so? You're old enough that I suppose you should be good at it by now."

"*Should* be?" Zahir brushed his lips over hers. "Oh, little sparrow, I don't even have to touch you to get you off."

"Wow. The arrogance." Ezra rolled her eyes. "Whatever you say, my king."

"You want proof?" Zahir said, his hand slipping around her throat. "Your heart is suddenly racing. I think it means you want proof."

Ezra bit her lip, and his dick hardened. "Go on then. If you think you can."

Zahir moved off her before he never moved again. A chair appeared on the other side of the rugs, and he sat, facing her. He wasn't going to miss a second of this.

CHAPTER SIXTEEN

*E*zra didn't know if Zahir was only teasing her, but she didn't expect him to start following through with it. Her heart was a drumbeat in her ears as he sat down on a chair and crossed his legs.

Ezra opened her mouth to sass him when she felt his power move against her throat in a hot caress. The words died in her mouth as the invisible tongues of magic slid down her breasts and popped open the buttons of her shirt.

"Did you think I was bluffing?" Zahir asked innocently. His eyes were glowing bronze, the inferno of his magic barely leashed. She could feel it oozing out of him, teasing her magic like its master teased her body. "Do you want me to stop, my little sparrow?"

"No..." she gasped, unable to do anything else.

Zahir smiled like a tiger with a mouse between its paws. The hot, invisible fingers tugged her bra down, and a tongue licked over her nipple. Ezra's back curved, and her hand slid down the button of her jeans.

"No, no. If I don't get to touch, you don't get to touch." Zahir made a small gesture with one finger, and hands gripped her wrists, pinning them to the soft cushions beneath her.

Ezra squirmed, but she didn't ask to be let go. Letting him have control made her feel a deep sense of relief that she hadn't felt since she learned of her father's death. She didn't want to be in control of anything just for a night.

"More," she begged. The invisible mouth on her nipple sucked harder, and then another appeared on her other breast until her entire chest was getting kissed over and over again. Ezra couldn't breathe as the feeling of multiple tongues started to slide over her skin.

Zahir was watching every little gasp and groan she made. "Can I remove those jeans?" he asked, his dark eyes flaring bronze.

Ezra nodded, unable to form words as her body drowned in pleasure. With a short snap of his fingers, Zahir's magic ripped her jeans off until she was only in her panties. She was glad that they were one of her nicer pairs.

"Fucking gorgeous," Zahir whispered and gripped the arms of his chair.

Warm hands glided up the insides of her thighs, gently brushing over her pussy, but not lingering. Ezra squirmed, biting her lip hard so she wouldn't beg. Her whole body was being stroked and kissed and sucked. The stars above her were spinning as she struggled against the invisible bonds holding her.

If this is what he could do without even touching her, she couldn't imagine what it would feel like to have his heat and body on top of her.

Curls of glittering bronze magic whispered against her skin like smoke before slipping underneath the edge of her panties.

Ezra couldn't look away as they slowly explored her. The hands on her legs spread her wider, and the bronze wisps trailed over her pussy. He didn't remove her panties, but he was watching her like he could see everything anyway. A trickle of sweat slid between her breasts and down her stomach before an invisible mouth licked it.

"Please," she whispered.

"Release your magic, sparrow. I want to feel it against mine when you come undone for me," Zahir replied, his voice a husky demand.

Ezra could barely think straight, but she reached inside of her and let her magic rise up within her. Zahir hissed as it sparked against him.

"That's it. Fuck, I could get addicted to this feeling. To seeing you all laid out for me like a fucking feast," he admitted, his eyes glazing with burning desire of his own. The bronze whispers of his magic spread her pussy wider before another lapped at her like a tongue. Ezra had never felt anything like it before, his magic sliding, teasing, taking, until she was weeping with pleasure.

"Zahir..." she moaned, and he doubled his efforts.

Her orgasm was all tangled up in their magic, making it feel like there was a living fire in her veins. Her whole body lifted as his magic fucked into her, and she cried out a wordless sound of pure ecstasy.

Ezra was exhausted, her body still throbbing all over in little electric shocks. She was floating, higher than any drug. Her fingers brushed against the soft carpet, and she realized she was *actually* floating.

She managed to lift her head and caught Zahir's eye. He was staring at her like he was shocked and in awe at the same time. His hands were trembling as he held one out and gently lowered her back to the pillows.

"Get over here and kiss me," Ezra whispered. She needed physical touch to ground her so she wouldn't feel like she was about to drift off the side of the roof.

Zahir got up slowly and dropped to her side. He was

frowning at her. "You are going to be so dangerous to me, my sparrow."

Ezra wanted to know what he meant by that, but before she could ask, he bent his head and gave her another of his deep, drugging kisses.

"Would you like me to return the favor?" she asked, biting her bottom lip. Zahir took her hand and placed it over his groin where the fabric was damp.

"You already did," he replied, his smile turning devious. "I'd be embarrassed if it didn't feel so good. You really are radiant when you're full of magic and coming with my name on your lips."

Ezra let out a breathless laugh. "Now I know the real reason I should fear the power of the djinn."

Zahir's eyes narrowed. "If any other djinn tries to touch you, I will annihilate them."

Ezra rolled her eyes and pinched his bearded chin. "Don't be possessive when we both know that you will lose interest in me at some point soon."

"My dear, when an old djinn gets interested in something, it is an absolute miracle. I wouldn't hold your breath thinking I'm going to let you out of my grip anytime soon," he replied so sincerely that she had to look away.

Ezra didn't know what to make of that or of the pleasure blooming in her chest that his words caused. She ran a hand down his back and curled into him.

"Whatever you say, my king," she replied, closing her eyes.

"I like when you call me that. Sleep, my sparrow. No one will harm you while I'm here," Zahir said, and she could've sworn he kissed her head.

Ezra drifted off to the sound of his heartbeat and dreamed of deserts under the burning stars.

CHAPTER SEVENTEEN

*E*zra was buried deep in one of Judah's more recent work journals when there was a knock at the door. Her mind took a few moments to register the sound.

Judah had fallen deep into his own brilliant world since Ezra had been in Florence. He had become almost manic with his study, including translating an ancient Egyptian spell that had been discovered by an archaeologist friend of his in Edfu.

You could ask Zahir or Ashirah to tell you what it says.

The thought sent a magical twinge of excitement through her. Being friends with djinn could have some amazing benefits in her field of study. Maybe she wouldn't be working in clubs forever. She had spent the morning doing her best *not* to think of Zahir and the night before. She had woken to breakfast and sunflowers, and her heart had...

Another bang at the door.

"Coming!" Ezra shouted and hurried through the house. She pulled open the door and found a tall blond-haired man waiting for her.

"Can I help you?" she asked.

His pale blue eyes lit up with warmth. He looked her over.

"You are Ezra? I have been sent by Zachariah to assess where your studies are at." He had a thick accent that she didn't recognize. He was polite enough not to storm in like Zachariah had, so Ezra tried for politeness.

"Sure, come on in," she said and let him through the wards. "Please excuse the mess in the study. My father was brilliant at many things, but housekeeping wasn't one of them."

"I am yet to meet a neat genius," he replied. He was letting off a low magical hum, so Ezra knew he was a mage, but she couldn't guess what he specialized in.

"I've been going through his recent work for the Cabal, trying to piece together the last six months and get into his head space," she said and blew out a frustrated breath. "He seemed to be less focused than usual."

"And the work on the golems?" he asked with a lift of an ashen brow. "The other *shem* didn't work in your golem like Zachariah hoped."

"Damn, that changes things." Ezra hesitated. She might not be able to fool this man like she had Zachariah and the artist. "It's hard to follow Judah's train of thought. He seems to have scattered the work across three different journals and—"

Pain burst through Ezra's nose, and she cried out in surprise and clutched at it. The mage followed up his strike with another to her right eye, and she sank to the floor.

"W-What the hell? I'm trying to help…" she said.

Blood was gushing out of her nose, and her eyes were watering. She needed to get up, but her head wasn't clear enough. The mage kicked her hard, her rib cracking.

"I've been sent here to motivate you, Miss Eliyahu. You don't seem to realize the urgency or the seriousness of your situation." The mage smiled down at her, and his wrists split open, bright magical ropes coming out of them. "But you will."

Ezra screamed as the ropes whipped out against her back,

splitting the fabric of her shirt and bra and exposing her. She curled into herself, trying to hide her nakedness.

"S-Stop," she begged. The mage didn't listen to her, and the whips came down again.

Ezra screamed with every strike. It could have lasted a minute or an hour. Her voice went hoarse. Everything was burning, and she couldn't breathe.

"I'll be back tomorrow. You had best get to work," the mage said, and then he was gone, the door shutting behind him.

"Help... Zahir..." Ezra cried, unable to move, her body shutting down.

Magic moved towards her like a vortex. It rolled towards her in a dark shape, blurred by her tears and blood. She held a shaking hand out to it. "Zahir..."

"Ezra?" a deep voice said then swore in another language. "It's Asim. I've got you, sweet butterfly."

"Zahir," she sobbed.

"I'll get you to him. It's going to be okay," Asim promised. Ezra couldn't feel her body as she was lifted up into the big djinn's arms, and she cried out. "Hush, now. I'll take you to the king. And the Creator help us all."

CHAPTER EIGHTEEN

Zahir couldn't concentrate on what Lorenzo Tera, the Coins representative, was saying about the foundation works that they were currently completing in the lower areas of the city. He had his indigo journal with him, and his thumb kept idly rubbing over the small sparrow that had been pressed on the bottom corner.

He hadn't received any messages from Ezra, and he was trying his best not to let it bother him. He hadn't wanted to wake her, so he had left her wrapped in a blanket on the roof. He'd erected a tent over her to make sure the weather didn't bother her and had left her a platter of tea and breakfast. He had also made sure that there were blooming sunflowers because she said that she loved them so much.

You are being pathetic, he told himself. Maybe he should have woken her.

It was late afternoon; she would have definitely woken by then. He opened the notebook again, still nothing. Zahir's pen hovered over the page. He pulled back, not wanting to smother her. Ezra was a grown woman. She would message him when she was ready to.

Arkon nudged him with his foot, rousing him from his thoughts. He tapped some writing on his notebook. *Stop thinking of your mage.*

Zahir ignored him. Arkon was in no position to give advice when it came to obsessing over mages. He rubbed at his chest, trying to relieve the strange ache that appeared there. Was he... having feelings? It was so, so dangerous for him to become attached to something so fragile as a human. He thought of her crooked smile and the way her mouth felt on his.

Zahir tried not to let his imagination run too wild. He was still embarrassed that he had come untouched, just by feeling the echoes of her orgasm through their magic. Fuck, she was so... He didn't have the words.

His thumb ran over the sparrow imprint again. He hoped she was okay. He didn't like this feeling in his chest. It was almost a panicky sensation that something was wrong, but he had no evidence to back it up.

Zahir started as Gio dropped his book on the table loudly. "Okay, everyone, we are done for the day," he said, getting to his feet. He gave Zahir a suspicious look. Zahir smiled innocently. He wasn't going to worry Gio about golems being sold to the Varangians without the evidence needed to take care of the problem. The Doge had enough to worry about.

"What's wrong with you today?" Arkon asked once they left the council chambers.

"I don't know. Something feels off." Zahir shook his head. "It's nothing."

Arkon didn't look convinced. "Well, here is something that might lift your spirits. My Ravens have identified the men in the pictures you gave Stella. The older one is Zachariah Todesa, and the artist is Giuseppe Zacuto."

Zahir smiled. "That *is* good news. I trust that they are running down all of their known associates."

"Every one down to the members of their book clubs. We

will find out who is behind this Cabal in no time." Arkon nudged him with his shoulder. "What's going on with you and Ezra? Stella is very taken with her."

Zahir shook his head. "You are like a gossipy old *nonna*."

"I'm the spymaster. Gossip is my trade. Come on, tell me," Arkon coaxed.

"She's disrespectful, sassy, and the most outstanding kisser," Zahir relented. "I like her, Arkon, and I don't know if that's a good thing or not."

Arkon smiled softly. "It is. Jaded old bastards like us find it hard to like anyone. We've seen the worst of humanity, so when we find a person we genuinely like, it throws us out of balance."

"That's remarkably insightful," Zahir teased. He frowned and rubbed at his chest as the pressure increased again.

Arkon noticed the movement. "What is it? Are you hurt?"

"I don't know. I have the strangest feeling that something is wrong, like panic."

"We are in the middle of a war and dealing with traitors. Something is always wrong," Arkon replied and frowned. "Do djinn get heartburn?"

"It's not funny. Something is really..." Zahir gasped as his chest squeezed tight. He started to sag and Arkon caught him up.

"Zahir! Breathe!" the sorcerer commanded.

Zahir tried to, but everything hurt. He had never felt anything like it before. He gasped in and out until the pressure eased a little. His magic was flaring, and he fought to keep hold of his physical body.

"I-I'm okay," he said to Arkon, who was flapping about like a frightened bird.

"You are not okay! What the fuck?! Djinn don't have heart attacks!" he replied.

"Lower your voice, and stop making a scene," Zahir snapped.

Arkon lifted him back to his feet and led him over to one of the marble railings.

The sorcerer looked spooked. "You completely blinked out of there for a second. Are you sure you're okay? I can get Ashirah? Oh, look, here she comes now."

Zahir glanced up to see his second in command striding towards him. She looked grimmer than usual.

"Thank God you are here. He's losing it," Arkon told her, putting his hands on his hips. "He's hurt!"

"I am not. Stop being dramatic," Zahir complained.

"Ashirah, he collapsed!"

Ashirah placed a hand on Zahir's shoulder. "My king?"

"I'm fine. I just felt like my insides were being crushed for a moment. My chest has been hurting," Zahir told her.

Ashirah's frown deepened. "In the last hour or so?"

"Yes. How did you know?" Zahir asked in alarm. "What are you doing here? What's happened?"

Ashirah gripped his shoulders. "I don't want you to panic, but a man came to visit Ezra. We don't know if he was Cabal or not."

Zahir sat on the marble railing. He was shaking and couldn't stop. "What did he do? Spit it out already!"

"I don't know all the details. Asim was watching her and saw them arrive. He heard screaming, but you ordered us not to interfere. He didn't know whether he should go in or not." Ashirah's voice hadn't lost any of its steadiness. "After the stranger left, Asim went in to check on Ezra. He couldn't handle it, so he disobeyed you and went inside. Whoever the guy was, he messed her up, Zahir. She's hurt."

"Did Asim get a good look at the guy? He could be a part of this Cabal," Arkon asked. Zahir was no longer listening. His body locked up in fury, flames bursting along his skin.

"Where is she?" he demanded, his voice going metallic with magic and rage.

"Asim took her to the boat. He didn't know what else to do," Ashirah said.

Zahir blinked out of existence and shot through the ether. He'd left the boat in Cannaregio that day because he'd felt like walking. He landed on the deck and re-materialized, wreathed in flames. The djinn on deck scattered except for Asim, who was guarding the door to the lower cabins.

"Where is she?" Zahir snarled.

Asim lowered his eyes in deference. "I placed her in your chamber, my king. She was attacked and called out for you. I didn't… I didn't know what else to do."

Zahir pushed some of his rage down and patted him on the arm. "You did the right thing to bring her here."

Asim looked up at him, his eyes dark with anger. "I should've done something sooner."

"It's okay. I'm not mad at you," Zahir tried to reassure him.

Asim stepped away from the door. "But you will be."

Zahir moved into the cabin, through his office where he received petitioners, and into his private bed chambers. It was the one place he didn't allow anyone to enter. The roof was made of a mosaic of stained glass that made different colors shine all over it. Ezra was on the bed in a curled-up bundle, sobbing quietly with a stained sheet over her.

Zahir swallowed hard. As he moved closer, he saw what had upset his djinn. She was covered in bloody stripes from her neck to her ankles. He couldn't breathe again.

"Ezra?" he whispered, his voice cracking. "Sparrow?"

Ezra turned towards him and showed him her busted face. One eye was completely swollen shut. "T-They realized the *shem* in the other g-golem didn't work," she sobbed.

Zahir cursed low and long before lifting the sheet away. "We need to heal you right away before this becomes infected."

"T-They will know you helped me…"

"I don't fucking care, Ezra!" Zahir snapped before rubbing

his hands over his face. "Any decent med-mage in the city could do as much."

He was so beyond angry that the ship was shuddering slightly, reacting to his mood. He took some deep breaths to try to still himself. He had been tortured and whipped many times while he had been enslaved. He knew exactly what she was going through, and he was desperately trying not to let it trigger him. He had to heal her, and then he would unleash hell on the fucking men responsible.

Zahir touched a bare space on Ezra's shoulder and drained the pain from her body. Ezra gasped, her body twitching as pain rose up above her in a twisted ball of blackness. Zahir incinerated it, burning it away until there wasn't anything left.

"T-Thank you," she said and sniffed hard.

Zahir stroked her hair. "Hush now. Let me heal you. Then you can tell me who did this to you so I can pull their limbs off one at a time."

"You're a little scary, you know that, right?" she said, her busted lips lifting in a smile.

"Yes, and I'm not to be fucked with, so you be a good girl and rest for me," he replied, his gruffness out of sheer self-defense. Ezra turned away from him so he could see the full extent of her back. She had been whipped, that much he was certain of, but he had never seen whip marks that were scorched into flesh.

"What did they use on you so I know what weapon of choice I'm going to kill them with?" he asked, placing his finger on the first deep slash and sending healing magic through it.

"He didn't carry one. These long, electrified cords came out of his wrists and struck at me. They burned my clothes off. My face was done with his fists. He caught me off guard. He said he'd come on behalf of the Cabal and asked to see the drawings I was working on. Perfectly pleasant. Then without losing his smile, he laid into me," Ezra said, her voice steadier now that the pain was gone. "They must have told him that if I could think properly, I'd be able to fuck him up with magic. It was smart in a sadistic way. He said that he'd been sent to motivate me because the other golem stopped working."

Zahir could hardly breathe through his anger. "He didn't happen to be stupid enough to give you his name?"

"No, but he wasn't Venetian. He had a strange thick accent and spoke English," Ezra replied.

"That's something we can work with. Asim saw his face, so he won't be able to hide from us for long." Zahir healed another two deep slashes until they were pink scars. They could be healed entirely, but affordable med-mages didn't do cosmetic work. Once the Cabal members were swinging from the gallows, he would wipe away every horrible mark that they left on her.

"I'm so sorry this happened to you," Zahir said, his chest aching again. "I should have known they would hurt you." They had already done it, after all. That hadn't left marks, and Zahir hated himself for allowing her to be in harm's way.

Once the last wound was healed on her back, Zahir draped a gold and indigo robe over her and helped her sit up. Ezra looked up at him, her face a swollen mess.

"I must look worse than I feel," she said, staring up at him.

"You are still beautiful," he replied honestly.

Ezra huffed a laugh. "You just can't help being a flirt, can you?"

"You make it easy." Zahir stroked her cheek and focused his power into gently healing the swelling and the cracked nose and cheek bone underneath. Once it was done, Ezra moved her jaw from side to side and touched her nose.

"You really do have magic hands. I don't suppose you have a bathroom in here?" she asked.

Zahir nodded. "Stay here. I'll run the bath for you." He went through a narrow door and into the bathroom. He turned on the taps of the deep copper tub and tipped in some salts. He felt so fucking helpless. He grabbed one of the plush orange towels and screamed into it.

"Did that make you feel better?" Ezra asked from behind him. He started and turned, shoving the towel aside.

"Not really," he admitted. His insides were shredded, and the more he looked at her still bloody face, the more irrational he felt. "Let me get out of your way."

Ezra caught him by the shirt, stopping his retreat. She lifted up on her toes and placed a gentle kiss on his lips.

"Thank you for everything," she whispered before letting him go. "Especially the sunflowers."

Something cracked inside of him. He wanted to bundle her up in his arms and never let her go.

"Stay in it as long as you need to. I'll get some food," he said and got out of there before he lost his mind.

CHAPTER NINETEEN

*E*zra's body might not have been in pain any longer, but her muscles and skin throbbed with the memory of it. She sat in the deep bathtub that smelled of jasmine and slowly washed the blood from her freshly healed skin. She was shaking in the hot water, shivering like she would never feel warm or safe again. Tears fell down her cheeks before she quickly washed them away.

For all of her magic and self-defense training, Ezra hadn't been ready for an actual attack. Ezra tried to push away the feeling of the whips of magic ripping into her, hoping that her trauma's response would make her forget.

Instead, she focused on the glittering, colorful roof above her. It was beautiful for purely aesthetic and not designed for practical purposes. It was very Zahir, like the rest of the bathroom. Rich, colorful towels, soaps, and artwork decorated the space, all chosen to complement the shining copper tub and fixtures.

Ezra went through the little soaps until she found one that smelled like her usual myrrh and scrubbed herself. The scars on her back felt tender from their healing, but not painful. No, he had pulled that clean out of her body like it was a loose tooth.

How does he contain such power? Logically, Ezra knew that djinn didn't just *have* magic; they *were* magic. She also knew that boats floated on water but didn't understand the how of it. Both djinn and boats were so common in Venice that she'd never really thought about it. She was thinking about it now.

Zahir had been a vortex of power when he'd landed on the ship. It had radiated through her bones and scorched her magic. Despite the agony she was in, it had frightened her. It didn't make her want to run screaming away from him. No, it made her want to run screaming *towards* him. He made her feel safe, and logic said he was anything but.

Since magic had come flooding back into the world hundreds of years beforehand, it had become like another form of currency. Whoever had the most magic had the most power. The djinn—Zahir alone—could have snapped his fingers and ruled the Republic. He didn't though, and neither did any of the other djinn. He was their king because he was the strongest and kept them all in line.

And you almost fucked him on a rooftop after teasing him for fun. You really are a fool.

Ezra had woken after the best night's sleep in months. She had blushed when she realized one of the tattooed lines marking the nights of their bargain had vanished. She had eaten the breakfast he'd left her, sheltered in a tent that looked like it belonged in the Sahara somewhere. Her heart had gone erratic at the pots of sunflowers all over the roof. For a moment, she had been so happy and in awe of magic like she was a little girl again.

Ezra had planned to do some work before messaging Zahir, and then her entire day had become pain and fear. She swallowed down a mouthful of bitter tears.

You're safe now, she tried to tell herself. But for how long? She didn't know how to go home and feel like she wouldn't be attacked again. Ezra would change all the wards as soon as she went back and would hope that they were strong enough to keep people out.

Ezra could feel the ghost of the manacles around her wrists, and new resentment flowed through her. She would do everything she could to find her way to the Cabal and get her freedom. If there was any justice in the world, she would watch them hang and spit on their corpses.

When the bath grew cool, Ezra stepped out of it, dried herself with one of the thick towels and put the gold and indigo robe back on. She wanted to feel like she had that morning, in awe of magic and the Djinn King who created it. She didn't want to feel afraid.

Ezra stepped out of the bathroom and found Zahir sitting in a plush chair next to a table laden with food. He looked furious, with gold flickering in his eyes like a banked fire. As soon as he saw her, it faded out, and he smiled.

"Are you feeling any better?" he asked, holding a hand out to her. Ezra moved by his side, and he took her hands and kissed them.

"Thank you again for healing me," she said.

"Never thank me for that, sparrow. I'm so angry you had to go through that. I'm so sorry," he replied, resting his forehead against her stomach.

Ezra threaded her fingers through his dark hair. "It's not your fault. We will find these bastards, and I will get revenge," she replied, steel in her voice.

"That I will promise you with no bargain at all." Zahir pulled her gently into his lap before offering her a cup of tea. "Drink this. It will help with your blood loss and the adrenaline crash."

Ezra drank the dark tea and her insides stopped churning. "You are not like I imagined, you know that?"

Zahir smiled. "It's better, isn't it?"

"The ego is on point," she teased, and her heart lightened a little. She placed the empty teacup on the table. "I never expected you to be this kind."

"You are easy to be kind to." Zahir looked thoughtful. "I never expected to like you as much as I do. It's strange and vexing, but I can't seem to stop."

Ezra pressed a soft kiss to his cheek. "Don't stop."

Zahir's eyes heated before kissing her. His hands stroked feather light down her back before pulling her even closer. Ezra's hands went back to his thick hair, the silky strands so soft between her fingers. Her tongue stroked his lips, and he opened for her.

Ezra was burning up, and she didn't want it to end. Zahir's hands dropped to her ass, squeezing it as she ground against him. The night before, he hadn't physically touched her, and it had blown her mind. His actual hands on her made Ezra lose it altogether.

Zahir's hand slipped into her robe and cupped her breast. He groaned before pulling away from her so he could kiss his way down her throat.

"Are you sure you want this, Ezra?" he asked softly.

"Yes. I need you," she said, hands in his shirt. "Make me forget it all. Please, Zahir. I need to feel alive again."

"Your wish is my command." Zahir opened her robe, gently leaning her back so his mouth could suck on her brown nipple. Ezra moaned softly as another invisible mouth sucked on her other breast.

"Oh fuck, you're going to play those games too?" she gasped.

Zahir chuckled. "My darling, there are so many games I want to play with you." He opened up her robe so she was fully exposed to him. She tried not to squirm, fighting the urge to cover herself again. It wasn't that she hated her body, but the intensity of his gaze made her feel raw. His dark gaze was a hot touch as it traveled over her breasts, the roll of her belly, and down to her pussy.

Zahir leaned in to nuzzle her neck. "I honestly don't know where to start. Do you have a preference?"

"Anywhere," she whispered, her cheeks going red. "Everywhere."

"Hmm, how about here?" His fingers slid over the tops of her thighs before one knuckle brushed down her pussy. She whimpered, her legs tightening. Zahir chuckled, low and dirty. "My little sparrow is wet already." He moved his finger over her again, torturously slow, spreading her wetness in delicate patterns that had her hands gripping his shoulders.

"Holy fuck," she gasped.

Zahir only smiled and added a little more pressure. He was watching every one of her movements, figuring out what made her squirm and shake. Ezra's orgasm was shivering through her, the soft winding patterns making her body hum.

"So fucking good."

Zahir's eyes flashed with power. "Be a good girl and come for me."

Ezra was helpless under his command. She kissed him, smothering her cry of release against his lips.

"Such sweet sounds," he purred. He lifted his finger from her, admiring the glistening come on it before rubbing it on his lips and licking it. His eyes flashed. "I must have more."

Ezra clung to him as he stood, carrying her over to his bed and laying her down. She was still blissed out, content to let him do whatever the fuck he liked.

Zahir unbuttoned his shirt, and she got her first look at his gorgeous bare chest. It was well muscled in a lean, powerful way, his golden-brown skin covered in a fine dusting of black hair. Ezra noticed the scars on him and wondered what could possibly be powerful enough to mark a djinn.

Zahir stroked her from her lips, down her throat and

breasts. "So beautifully made. So much power in you. I want to tie you to this bed and never let you be in harm's way again."

"Don't you dare," Ezra replied with a smile. She didn't know how to take his soft, possessive threats or whether they were spoken in the heat of the moment.

He kissed her stomach, bringing her back to him. His hands widened her legs so he could move between them, kissing his way down. Zahir's hot mouth closed over her pussy, making Ezra bite her lip hard. Her fingers tightened on the sheets, needing something to hold on to as his pierced tongue flicked against her clit.

"Fuck... me..." she said breathlessly. Zahir didn't stop. His clever tongue danced, his fingers spreading her so he could move lower. Ezra didn't think she could handle much more. She was so wrong.

Zahir's tongue fucked into her, and she arched straight off the bed. He chuckled against her, his hands gripping her ass and holding her up to his mouth. A pillow appeared underneath her.

"What a delicious sight you make like this," Zahir mused, his fingers tracing over her legs. "Maybe I could keep you like this when I'm doing paperwork, so I have something worth looking at."

"You seriously overestimate my ability to stay still," Ezra replied, her voice shaky.

Zahir hummed. "I could always tie you in place with silk scarves." Ezra's core burned at the thought. She'd never been into any form of bondage, but if Zahir did it...

Zahir seemed to know exactly what she was thinking because his grin widened. "I think my little sparrow likes that idea," he said before licking the inside of her thigh. "Perhaps another time. I want you just like this right now." He put his mouth back over her clit and sucked hard. Ezra cried out, her toes curling tightly into the sheets, and she lifted her pelvis higher.

"Oh god, please just fuck me," she begged.

Zahir released her. "All in good time. You wanted me to make you forget. By the time I'm done with you, you won't even remember your own name."

Zahir moved back and undid his pants, letting them slide to the floor. Ezra's eyes went to his cock and grew wide. He was long and hard and gorgeous, like she had suspected, but he was also pierced. A small golden bar shone through his tip.

"Like what you see?" he asked teasingly and gave himself a few strokes.

Ezra nodded. "I need a closer look."

"Read my mind," he said. He surprised her by climbing onto the bed and placing his legs on either side of her head. "Better?"

Ezra nodded and licked the tip of his dick. "Doesn't that hurt?"

"No, *habibi*. It feels amazing. You're going to think so too when it's buried inside of you," Zahir said with a wicked grin.

Ezra opened her mouth for him, and he slid inside. Under his instruction, she tugged and toyed with the piercing until a fine sheen of sweat covered him. She couldn't look away as he fucked her mouth, his body moving sinuously like he knew exactly how to make it look as erotic as possible.

"Fuck, Ezra, your mouth is so good," he said, his hands gripping the headboard, and looked down at her. "I want to make you feel good too." Ezra gasped around him as she felt hands moving all over her again. Her hands gripped his thighs, and he pulled free of her mouth. "Breathe, my Ezra."

"I can feel you everywhere," she said, eyes blowing wide. Hot mouths covered her breasts, sucking her as others appeared between her thighs.

"That's right. I'm going to have all of you tonight. I'm going to ruin you for anyone else, and I'm too selfish to care," Zahir said, running a thumb over her wet lips. "Now, open up for me so I can come down your pretty throat."

Ezra opened her mouth, and he thrust inside. She was burning up, her pleasure reaching another place. She gripped Zahir's ass, holding onto him and trying not to lose her mind. The invisible hands and mouths caressed her breasts, her pussy, her ass, and everywhere else until she was coming again. At the same time, Zahir cried out, and her mouth flooded with come. She swallowed it down as he moved back.

Zahir's expression was wild as he kissed her deeply, like he needed to taste himself in her mouth. He was still impossibly hard as he moved over her.

"Now, I will fuck you," he growled and pushed inside of her with one hard thrust. Ezra couldn't stop the sounds coming out of her as he pounded into her. Her nails clawed down his back and sides, spurring him on. Her insides were liquid fire, and she let him set the pace, unable to do anything but hang on.

Ezra's magic flared unbidden, and Zahir let out a breathless laugh above her. He brushed her tangle of curls from her face.

"Yes, Ezra, let the power be free. Let me in," he begged, and her magic obeyed. It crashed into him, making them both gasp. "Fucking perfect. Yes, more Ezra." Something inside of her cracked open and magic roared out from behind it. Strength infused her, and she flipped Zahir onto his back. He stared up at her with a shocked expression, his black hair a wild mess around him. "What are you?"

Ezra didn't answer—couldn't—she needed him, and that was all she knew. Zahir laughed wildly and gripped her ass hard enough to bruise.

"Take it all, ruin me," he said, and Ezra did. Her fingers clawed into his chest as she rode his cock, moving until it hit the perfect spot inside of her. Hands gripped her bouncing tits while Zahir's own moved to stroke her clit.

Ezra was possessed, a voice in her trying to make her realize that this would drive her to madness. She pushed it away and let the magic and pleasure and Zahir's beautiful smiling face demolish her. She screamed his name as her orgasm tore her in half.

Ezra blacked out, Zahir quickly sitting up and catching her before she fell backward. He kissed her back to consciousness, murmuring something in a language she didn't know. It sounded worshipful. She knew the feeling. She rested her face against his neck, trying to get enough breath in her lungs.

"Who… Who am I again?" she panted. Zahir kissed her shoulder, holding her tight to him.

"Mine," he said, lifting her chin with his finger. His eyes were all wild djinn, magic, and lust. "That's who you are. You're mine."

CHAPTER TWENTY

*Z*ahir lay stretched out on his silk sheets, with one hand slowly trailing along Ezra's bare hip.

"I have a question," she said sleepily. "When all of your invisible hands touch me, do you feel it, or is it just for me?"

Zahir propped his head up with a hand. "I feel it as if I'm touching you myself. I could feel my mouth licking you as you licked me."

"Wow, I am going to have to tell Stella that her friend was right."

Zahir lifted a brow. "About what?"

"That sex with a djinn is transcendental," Ezra replied, her cheeks still flushed with color.

"My dear, sex with *you* is transcendental. It has been a long time since I have felt so much." Zahir's fingers trailed down her back and over the scars marring it.

"Is that a good thing or a bad thing?" Ezra asked.

"Honestly? I'm not sure. For example, it's made me feel like I need to wrap you in feather blankets and let nobody near you ever again." Zahir said it lightly, but he felt anything but. His whole body was aching in a way he had never experienced before. He couldn't get close enough to her. He felt a reckless need for her that he knew was unnatural.

He needed advice but wasn't sure who to go to about it. It wasn't as if he hadn't been obsessed with a human before, but nothing like this. When her magic had plunged into him, he had felt her mark him on a molecular level.

Ezra's expression softened. "You know that I can't stay here. We have to find a way to end this with the Cabal and whoever that foreign mage was. I won't get those answers if you are coddling me."

Zahir's grip on her tightened. "I won't have you hurt again, Ezra. I can't bear it, and you shouldn't have to."

Ezra kissed the tip of his nose. It was a sweet, affectionate gesture that he wasn't sure he deserved. Sex he could always do; affection was another matter entirely.

"Give me two days. If I don't have the answers for you, we forget the whole thing, and you can do it your way," she said.

"You don't have to prove to me how brave you are."

"It's not about bravery. It's about revenge. I need to take them down for everything they have done to my family. They broke my father's brain before they smashed him like he was worth nothing. I wouldn't be able to live with myself if I didn't try, Zahir. Surely you can understand that."

Zahir didn't want to fight with her. "I do understand. I am still too angry to agree to anything right now. Stay with me tonight, and I will consider it in the morning."

"A compromise from the King of the Djinn? No one would believe it." Ezra's smile was sweet and teasing. He couldn't resist leaning in to kiss it.

"Surely you should know by now that nearly everything that is said about me is a rumor? It's an elaborate armor, designed to let everyone think I am something that I'm not."

Ezra pretended to look shocked. "So you're telling me you

aren't a sex god because I have it on good authority that you are."

"That one is true," he replied, kissing her again.

Ezra combed her fingers through his hair. "You are definitely sweeter than I thought you would be."

"Don't tell anyone. I need to keep a healthy fear of me in the public."

Ezra laughed softly and rolled onto her back to gaze up at the colorful roof above her. "Why did you do your roof this way? It is beautiful, but I doubt that it's practical."

Zahir contemplated lying to her because he didn't know how she would take the truth. He wanted her in his life, beyond the bargain that they had. He knew she was someone who valued honesty, and she deserved to know that he was quite mad.

"I have been imprisoned many times in my long life," he began, turning to look at the colors above him. "Putting my kind into vessels to grant wishes, unfortunately, was a very true reality for many of us. The last time I was imprisoned, it was by a Roman priest of Jupiter in Baalbek. He trapped me in a colorful glass jewelry box. The effort of the magic killed him, and I was stuck in that jewelry box for centuries. This ship is a sanctuary for me. The place that I go to when I feel over-whelmed."

Ezra placed a hand on his cheek. "It reminds you of being in the box?" she guessed.

Zahir nodded. "Some days, all the power and all the freedom in the world is suffocating. It helps me re-center and makes everything feel smaller again. I don't know if that makes any sense."

"When I was a little girl, and I used to feel that way, I used to hide in cupboards," Ezra admitted. "I understand probably more than you think. If this makes you feel safe, who am I to judge you? We all need somewhere that makes us feel that way."

Zahir rested his hand over her beating heart. "Just when I think I can't adore you more, you just accept this part of me."

"I wish I could believe you when you say things like that," Ezra whispered. She sounded so sad that it broke his heart a little. She lifted her arm where there was only one mark of the bargain remaining. "Until this is gone, I won't ever know if it's the bargain making you say them or if you actually mean them."

Zahir wanted to argue with her that bargains didn't work that way. He saw in her eyes that she would never believe him. It hurt a lot more than he thought it would, but he accepted it.

"I respect your honesty, and I do understand why you would think that way." Zahir leaned in until his nose touched hers. "But believe me, when I tell you, when that mark is gone, I am not going to disappear. You and I are caught up in something that I don't understand yet. I am not going anywhere until I know why you make me feel this way."

"And what if I don't want a big, possessive djinn bossing me around?" Ezra asked. She was teasing him, but the thought of being separated from her didn't go down well.

Zahir's hand closed gently around her throat, and he leaned in the kiss her. "I think you secretly like me bossing you around, especially when you're naked."

Ezra's fingers twisted in his hair. "It's not a secret. Sex is one thing, but know this, King of the Djinn. I am not your subject."

"And I would never want you to be. While you are in my bed, you are under my protection. If there is a repeat of what happened to you today, I will be a very bad djinn to whoever is responsible." He didn't disguise the threat in his voice. He didn't want to frighten her, but when they found the foreign mage, all that was going to be left of him when Zahir finished was going to be pink mist.

"No one has ever protected me, not even my parents." Ezra kissed him rough and needy. "Is it wrong that I find it so fucking hot when you talk like that?"

"There is nothing wrong with it. You are my sweet sparrow, and no one is going to hurt you again," he swore. He rolled her over and pulled her up against him as a little spoon. Ezra took his hand and guided it between her thighs. Zahir took the hint and palmed her pussy.

"I knew you liked me being possessive," he purred in her ear. He shifted so he could have one hand still closed around her throat. He needed to feel her fluttering pulse beneath his fingers.

Ezra slid her leg over his to give him better access. She was still wet from their last round of lovemaking, but that didn't bother him in the slightest. He loved that he could feel his come still dripping out of her. It made him feel more than a little possessive.

"You look so beautiful when you are needy. It makes me want to tease you until you get down on your knees and beg for me," he whispered and gently licked her ear.

A mirror appeared on the other side of the bed, angled to show Ezra naked. Zahir was a shadow behind her, his darker tanned hand between her thighs.

"Look at yourself. Look how gorgeous you are when you are unraveling for me," he said. Ezra's eyes opened, and she saw the mirror and his hand.

"Oh..." she whispered but didn't look away.

Zahir pressed two fingers inside of her, working her open. When she was squirming and ready for him, he flipped her onto all fours.

Ezra's eyes looked back at him in the mirror, burning with desire. Her luscious ass was in the air, and he guided his aching cock into her. She was so soft and hot and slick, he couldn't get enough. He wanted to fuck her slowly and couldn't.

"Yes, Zahir, harder," she pleaded. His lovely Ezra didn't want to be fucked sweetly. She was everything he needed.

Zahir spread her so he could watch himself disappear into

her. It was too much and not enough. He couldn't get close enough.

"Fuck, you are a marvel. I don't want to ever stop fucking you. You feel so good wrapped around me." Zahir had caught on that she liked to be praised and wanted to give her whatever she needed. He grabbed a handful of her hair and leaned over her. "Do you like being good for me?"

"Yes, my king," Ezra gasped. She clawed up his sheets and cried out, her pussy gripping him hard as she came. Zahir couldn't hold back any longer. He pulled her tight against him, crying out her name as he filled her with come. They collapsed on the sheets, panting for breath and utterly spent.

"You are going to be so bad for my health," Ezra said, trying to get her breath back.

"Or really good for it," Zahir laughed softly and pulled her over his chest.

CHAPTER TWENTY-ONE

*E*zra woke the following day to the smell of coffee and something strangely sweet, like tobacco and incense. She wasn't sore like she had been expecting to be. Her body was soft and languid, her muscles deliciously tired of a night of excellent sex.

You can't hide in this bed forever. She wished she could. She rubbed at her face and realized there was only one mark left on her arm. The magic of the bargain had done its work. She tried not to panic at the thought of having one more night with him. Something was raw and open inside of her, and she didn't know how to close it up again.

Ezra sat up and spotted Zahir's bare brown back on the other side of the room. He was sitting on a cushion in a loose pair of black silk pants, drinking coffee, smoking a hookah, and toying with black stones spread out on a low table. She pulled on her robe and went to join him.

"Ah, she wakes," Zahir said, pulling her down into his lap and giving her his coffee.

Ezra glowed with a strange pleasure. She had worried the previous night that it was sex that had made him affectionate. It made her dangerously pleased that he was being so comfortable with her. She sipped her coffee and hummed with happiness.

"What is all this?" she asked. The black stones were chips of obsidian in all different sizes. Glyphs she didn't recognize were carved into them. She could feel that they were magic, so she didn't dare touch them in case they zapped her.

"As you might be aware, my kind don't really use tarot cards. We use these instead." Zahir held one out to her. "Instead of showing us one future, a practiced user can see as many futures as they like. It's a hard skill even for a djinn to master. They can get too many futures at once and get lost in them." He passed one to Ezra, and she held it gently in her palm.

"And what question are you putting to them?" she asked him.

Zahir tapped on the piece of notepaper he had on the desk beside it. On it was a letter saying two words, *Arrest them.*

"This is a letter to Arkon about the two Cabal members that we already know of. I am done waiting for them to reveal themselves. We take these two and see who scrambles out of their holes in a panic." Zahir kissed her shoulder. "I know you want to help, but this foreign mage troubles me greatly. Are you sure you don't recognize the accent that he had?"

Ezra shook her head. "No, nothing that I've heard before. It was thick. I haven't traveled too widely, but it's not even something I've heard in the marketplace when the merchants have come in." She curled further into Zahir just thinking about the cold, blue eyes of the mage and his happy smile as he made her scream.

"I won't let him or anyone else hurt you like that again," Zahir replied. He touched the letter, and it folded itself up into a bird before it burst into flames and flew away. "In a day's time, we will know everything we need to about this Cabal. I'm not above a bit of practical torture to get the information I need." He had a vicious look in his eyes that Ezra had never seen before.

"If they aren't a part of the Wands District, please don't upset the Doge on my behalf. Let his grand sorcerer take care of it." Ezra kissed the curve of his jaw. "I still don't know if the Cabal ended up with my father's sigil that could trap a djinn. I don't want you to be hurt."

"Trying to trap me will be the last dumb mistake they make," Zahir assured her. He smiled a crooked smile. "If they did, you would figure out a way to set me free anyway. You know sigil magic better than anyone. You would be able to figure out a way to fix what your father created."

Ezra grinned back. "You *hope* I could figure out a way to do it."

She toyed with the obsidian chip in her hand and felt it go warm. Her magic was tingling underneath it, and she quickly put it down. As she did, a vision struck her of Zahir screaming on a floor made of stone. Her hands were broken, and she was hanging from a roof. Ezra let out a startled cry and pulled back from the table.

Zahir cupped her face, his expression concerned as he stared deep into her eyes. "Are you okay, sparrow? What did you see?"

Ezra rubbed her eyes. "Nothing, I think. It just gave me a little shock, that's all."

If she told him, she didn't know if he would believe her. If she mentioned her being hurt again, he might follow through with his threat and keep her wrapped up in feather blankets. There was no way she could stop that future from happening if she was stuck inside the boat.

"You shouldn't have been able to infuse the chips with magic at all." Zahir touched the chip that she had held, frowning at it. "When this mess with the Cabal is over, we are going to look more into your magic, *habibi*."

"We? After this bargain is done, what makes you think that there will be a 'we'?" Ezra said, only half teasing. She was already feeling far too much when it came to him. She knew that only pain lay down that path, but she couldn't seem to stop listening to what her heart was saying.

Zahir tucked one of her curls behind her ear. "I see we are back to you thinking that I'm only behaving this way because of the bargain we struck. That's okay. I am immortal. I have a lot of time to prove to you all the ways that you are wrong about that."

But I am not. Ezra didn't say it, but she thought about it. What future could they really have? He would always be the king of the djinn long after her ashes were poured into the sea.

"I need to go home and start working on something to give to the Cabal. As lovely as it is, I can't hide here forever," she said.

"It's not hiding. You can lie in my lap while I feed you baklava and tell you stories of all my wonderful exploits," Zahir argued playfully.

Ezra tugged him down to kiss him. "It sounds lovely, but it is still a no, I'm afraid. It's not in my nature to run away from a fight. Give me two days. If we still have nothing at the end of them, then I promise I will do things your way, and you can feed me as much pastry as you like."

"You do realize you are trying to make a bargain with the king of bargains?" Zahir said with an amused quirk of his brow.

Ezra kissed him softly again, touching her tongue against his lips in a playful swipe. "Is that a yes, my king?"

Zahir let out a frustrated sound of defeat. "Fine. But you only get two days and not a second longer. I am all out of patience dealing with these assholes."

"Thank you, oh generous one," she said with a fond smile.

"You see now I just feel like you are mocking me."

Ezra laughed and gave his golden earrings a playful flick. "I wouldn't dream of it."

"I'll take you home, but not until I have one more taste of you," he purred into her ear, his hand sliding up a silk covered thigh.

"Really? You didn't get enough sex last night?" she laughed.

"I'm not going to see you for a whole day," Zahir complained and nipped at her throat. "And I want you to be able to feel me while I'm not there."

"We really need to talk about this possessive streak you keep showing," Ezra said, her breath catching.

"Do we? And why is that?" he asked.

"Because we are impossible, and you being possessive is ridiculous," Ezra admitted.

Zahir laughed a sinful chuckle and turned her head. "*Amore mio*, I am King of the Djinn. Nothing is impossible for me." He kissed her before she could argue, and she went soft in his arms. Maybe she was willing to believe the impossible, even if it was just for a morning.

CHAPTER TWENTY-TWO

*Z*ahir dropped Ezra off in her rooftop garden. One moment they were on his boat; the next they were amongst Lucia's orange trees.

"Please reset your wards today," Zahir said, putting his hands on her shoulders. "If they come to visit again, it will hold them off long enough to message me."

Ezra let out an exasperated huff. "I will. Please, don't worry. Arkon will arrest the other two as you said. They will probably be too busy to worry about me." Zahir looked like he was about to start arguing, so she rose on her tiptoes and kissed him.

"Have a good day," she said.

Zahir let her go. "I'll see you tonight."

"You will?" Ezra asked with a lift of a brow.

Zahir's eyes narrowed. "I will." He was gone before she could argue with him. Not that she wanted to. His bed was comfortable and came with mind-altering orgasms.

With a sigh, Ezra went into the house and down to the bathroom. Her hair was a complete riot, but she didn't have a bruise on her from the previous day. She had things to plan, and while Zahir was around, she couldn't concentrate in the slightest. She had wondered what it would be like to be the center of his attention, and now she doubted she would be able to date anyone normal again. Ezra made her morning shower a cold one.

Downstairs, she put coffee on before braving to step back into Judah's study. What remained of her clothes were bloody rags. Ezra sucked in a breath and put her head between her knees.

"You're okay, Ezra. He healed you. You're okay," she repeated over and over. "You have wards to fix." She took the crystal recording device from the office and set it up on the front door. She had foolishly forgotten to set it the previous day. If she was going to catch the foreign mage or any other visitors, it needed to be in a better place.

Once it was done, Ezra reset the wards. She wove in new sigils to keep out any other magic users, as well as normal humans. She ignored the sadness that seeped through her when the last of Judah's magic within them disappeared. She couldn't risk leaving any of it in place because he had allowed the Cabal members to be woven into them. It hurt to feel that part of him leave, but he was dead, and she was going to do everything she could not to end up the same way.

Ezra cleaned the study and burned sage and incense to clear the bad vibes the previous day had left. She turned on her father's record player and danced to some wild violin music he had left on it.

"Fuck you Cabal of the fucking Wise!" she shouted, needing to get it out of her system. She couldn't let her fear choke her out.

When Ezra had calmed a little, she began to draw pages upon pages of sigils. She let her mind go and her magic have free rein. She drew golems of different sizes and genders. She wrote formulas for magical clay and how to fuse magic to gold and silver.

She wrote and drew until her hands ached and her magic calmed. It had felt more erratic than usual after a night with Zahir. There was something about the magic of the djinn that made her power come alive and burn hot.

Ezra was about to go in search of food when there was a hard knock at her front door. One quick look and her stomach plummeted. The blonde mage from the previous day was on the other side of it. She went back to the study and grabbed the pages she had been working on.

Ezra made sure the device by the door was working before she opened it. The mage's pale eyes looked her over, and he smiled his infuriating smile.

"Miss Eliyahu, I trust you are well?" he said, his accent thick.

"No, thanks to you. I spent the night with a med-mage putting me back together," she replied. He pushed against her wards and narrowed his eyes.

"It was not the usual way I like to go about things, but my masters are impatient for results. My hands, like yours, are tied," he replied.

Ezra held up the wad of papers. "I have figured out what the Cabal wants to know, but I can't finalize it unless I see the golems myself."

"Why? It is my understanding that you were only creating the scrolls," he said, eyes narrowing.

"That's where we were all wrong. I need to see them, feel them. The magic in the clay speaks to me of the golem's soul, for lack of a better word. The *shem* act as a life force, and to get it to fuse properly with the host, they need to be tailor-made," Ezra tried to explain. She shoved the papers at him through the wards. He took them, running his finger over the back of her wrist. She pulled her hand back to safety. "It's all there in a theory version if they want to check it. If they want me to attempt an experiment, they will need to show me the others."

The mage looked at the papers, and Ezra could tell he had no idea how to read them. Good. She doubted the rest of the Cabal could either, if they were relying so heavily on her father's input.

"I will take this to them, and you will get your answer by nightfall." The mage poked at her ward, his magic pressing in and letting it zap him. He laughed. "It will only keep you safe for a day, Miss Eliyahu. Tomorrow, I will tear it down just to prove that you will never be safe from me."

Ezra folded her arms. "By tomorrow, I could be free of these slave bonds, and you will have no cause to come back."

The mage stepped closer, the wards humming in warning. "Perhaps I will return for my own pleasure. I liked the sounds of your screams."

"I was being polite yesterday when I let you in my house. That was my mistake and one I won't make again. If you decide to return here thinking I'm going to let you get me down like that again, you've got another thing coming." Ezra let her wild power shine in her eyes, trying to imitate Zahir's foreboding gaze. "I will destroy you, you sadistic little prick."

The man laughed and stepped back. "I'll see you soon, Miss Eliyahu."

Ezra slammed the door in his face. She waited until he was gone before she went back into the study and burst into tears. She shook, her back aching in memory. He couldn't get through the wards without serious effort, and she would instantly feel him tampering with them. The messaging journal rustled, and she hurried to open it.

Zahir's words appeared instantly. *Is everything okay over there?*

Ezra grabbed her pen, the tip hovering over the page. He had said he could feel when she was upset. If she told him about the mage, her plan would go to hell. She took a breath and wrote; *I am fine. I just accidentally tripped one of my father's spells on a book*

125

and it frightened me. She held her breath, waiting to see if he would believe her response.

So what are you wearing?

Ezra let out a laugh. *None of your business. Go and focus on your meeting.*

Ezra shut the book to keep her from flirting back with him. She chewed her lip, thinking over her plan. She would be stupid not to tell anyone about it, especially if the Cabal took her up on the offer to go to their workshop. She couldn't involve Zahir because he would either try to stop her or he would piss off the Doge by trying to take his anger out on people who weren't under his jurisdiction.

Ezra's fingers brushed over the Vianello Publishing stamp on her journal. Her face lit up into a smile. "Stella."

CHAPTER TWENTY-THREE

*T*he council wasn't meeting that day, and Zahir was relieved to have the day to try to get himself together. He was worried about Ezra, his growing feelings toward her, and the Cabal that wanted to sell them out to the Varangians. Really, the amount of traitors in the Republic was getting out of hand.

Zahir picked up the obsidian chip that still held the faint traces of Ezra's magic. It shouldn't have been possible. He needed answers, and there was only one djinn who he knew might have answers. Of all the djinn in the Republic, Zahir was the oldest. That didn't mean that other djinn in the world weren't older still.

Ashirah knocked on his cabin door before entering. She took in the tumbled bed and the smell of female perfume in the air.

"Should I ask?" she said, crossing her arms.

"Do you need to?" Zahir straightened his robes of red silk.

"She's a human, Zahir. Be careful with that old heart of yours," Ashirah replied, looking genuinely concerned.

Zahir wondered if he was that easy to read. "Maybe that's

been my problem lately, little sister. I forgot how painfully good it was to feel this way."

"And what feeling is that?" she asked innocently.

"To care." He was being tactful, but she saw through it. "I need to go and see the old king."

Ashirah didn't look pleased with that idea. Zahir knew that they used to be close, but he never had the balls to ask *how* close. All he knew was they had a falling out a thousand years ago and hadn't spoken since.

"Are you sure? He said he didn't want to be disturbed," she said coolly.

"I don't have a choice. Something strange is happening with Ezra. And before you start, I'm not talking about an obsession with something new and shiny. Her magic is so strange, and it concerns me." Zahir tucked the obsidian chip into his pocket. "I need advice. Will you look after the rabble for me today? I will be back at sundown."

"Of course I will. Be careful of him. The old ones are all insane, and him most of all."

Zahir kissed her cheek. "I'll give him your love, shall I?"

"He's never accepted it before, so I don't see the point in bothering," she said under her breath. "I'll make sure we have eyes on your girl while you are gone."

"Thank you, my sister," Zahir replied and vanished in a haze of red smoke.

ZAHIR HADN'T ALWAYS BEEN the king of the djinn. He had been offered the role by the previous one, who thought someone younger was needed. Karsudan had wanted to enjoy the return of magic in the world, and he'd had enough of keeping the unruly young djinn in line. Zahir sometimes wondered why he said yes to the job, but deep down he knew. He wanted a purpose, somewhere to belong, and to have a real home again. Venice seemed the answer in many way

Karsudan resided on an island near Cyprus. Unless you were a djinn, you could never find it. Karsudan knew most djinn hated water, except for the marids, so his chances of getting disturbed were slim to none.

Zahir didn't bother to announce himself before he teleported himself to Karsudan's villa. The old king would have told him to go fuck himself, and unfortunately, Zahir couldn't take no for an answer.

The wards let him through, and Zahir re-materialized under a palm tree in Karusdan's garden. Two large, black panthers were sunning themselves on the marble stones, and water was trickling from the fountains. The house before him was reminiscent of an ancient Arabian fairy tale palace, with a library Zahir loved to spend time in. It was so extensive, most of it was held in another dimension. Karsudan was a scholar, amongst other things, and all he wanted to do was read his many books, contemplate the stars and universe and their place in it.

Zahir let the sun and silence wash over him. The old djinn definitely knew what a retired king needed. Silence wasn't something Zahir got much of anymore.

"I thought I felt trouble heading my way," a deep bass voice called through the trees. Zahir found the massive djinn lounging in the shade in a dark purple sarong and nothing else. His curling dark hair was streaked in silver and hung to the center of his broad chest. He had a closely trimmed beard on the sides with a longer goatee decorated with small silver cuffs to match the silver studs up both of his pointed ears.

Karsudan's black eyes were as intimidating as ever as he looked Zahir over. He shut his book. "And what brings you to my doorstep, young one?"

He was the only one that could get away with calling Zahir 'young.' Zahir smiled and bowed to him in the old style.

"You seem to be enjoying retirement," Zahir commented and sat on a white wicker chair.

"I earned it." Karsudan glanced around. "Ashirah isn't with you?"

"No. She's in Venice," Zahir replied. Disappointment flashed on the other djinn's face, there and gone in a second. "She is well, Kar. You were right. She does make an excellent second in command."

Karsudan sighed. "She was a queen more than once. She can play the game better than anyone. What brings you here, Zahir?"

Straight to the point, as always.

"I've met a human girl. She has sigil power unlike anything I've ever seen. She is strong enough to be able to trap djinn," Zahir began.

Karsudan's eyes narrowed. "You should kill her."

"I know, but I... I can't. There's something strange about her. I need your knowledge." Zahir ended up telling him the whole muddled story. He gave Karsudan the obsidian chip that held her magic. The older djinn studied it for a moment before putting it in his mouth. Purple light flashed in his eyes, and he spat it back out. He took a deep drink from his wine cup before sparking up a small brown cigar. The scent of blue lotus filled the air, and Zahir smiled at the fact that both he and Ashirah smoked the same ancient blend.

"You have wandered into an ancient mystery indeed, my young friend," Karsudan finally said. He pulled on his goatee thoughtfully. "You said you felt her distress?"

"Yes. I've never had the tie of a bargain do that before," Zahir said.

"Hmm, it's because it's not bargain magic linking you," Karsudan said, having another draw of his cigar. "There were stories in the early times that when the Creator made djinn, it made us as a pair. That our magic would be able to be shared with another."

Zahir scoffed. "What? Like the shifters have mates?"

"Exactly like that. The beasts have a physical connection. The djinn are rare creatures of magic, flame, and air, so that is what binds us. I've never seen it happen with a human before."

"But you have with a djinn?"

Karsudan nodded. "Let's just say I have it on good authority that it can happen. I would bet my library that the girl Ezra has djinn in her bloodline. Test it. You will see that I am right. Djinn magic can sleep for generations before it awakens in the right child."

Zahir ran his hands through his hair, panic building inside of his chest. "So you're saying Ezra is my mate?"

"I don't like that word," Karsudan complained. "She is your consort in magic. It's why your power misbehaves when you are together. Have sex, you'll see what I mean." Zahir huffed out a breath, and Karsudan smirked. "Already, Zahir? You waste no time."

"She doesn't have it to waste. She's not djinn. She won't live forever," Zahir replied.

Karsudan hummed thoughtfully. "You could bind yourself to her. It would give her immortality as long as it was in place."

"She might not want it. Ezra is very much her own person," Zahir replied.

Karsudan chuckled. "If your skills as a lover are so terrible that she would say no, then you don't deserve her."

"I don't deserve her anyway."

"On that, we can agree." Karsudan lifted his wine up to him. "I bid you good luck. If you can convince her to take the chance on what's left of your heart, bring her here. I'll officiate the binding to make sure you don't screw it up."

Zahir laughed. "Thank you, Ancient One. I might even be able to convince Ashirah to come with us as a witness."

Karsudan's eyes softened. "I would like that, but we all know it's not in the Star of Nineveh's nature to be told what to do. She knows where to find me. She always does."

"One day, you two are going to tell me whatever the fuck happened to cause this rift between you," Zahir replied.

"Oh? And how will you do that, little flame?" Karsudan teased. Zahir knew there was no point in trying to argue with him. Karsudan could squash them all like bugs. He was the closest to a living god that the djinn had.

Zahir rose to his feet and bowed deeply. "Thank you for your advice and knowledge."

"You're welcome." Karsudan tossed the obsidian chip to him. "Don't waste this chance to claim your consort, Zahir. You won't get another."

Zahir smiled his most carefree smile. "I won't. I want her too much."

He only needed to convince Ezra to want him back.

CHAPTER TWENTY-FOUR

*T*he Vianello Publishing House was a short ferry ride down the Grand Canal to Dorsoduro. Ezra had felt a djinn following her, and the tension in her shoulders after the mage's visit had eased a little. Zahir was keeping his promise to watch over her.

Ezra had dressed and put on makeup to ensure she looked presentable when she arrived at the publishing house's door. The district was Coins, so it was mostly humans and earth mages, but houses on the Grand Canal were expensive no matter what district you were in. It made her put in the extra effort, especially because Stella was no longer a Vianello. She was an Aladoro, and that meant something in Venice.

Ezra was shown upstairs by a helpful woman with a round face. Stella was in an office, arguing with an older man about a new shipment. She looked up and saw Ezra, and her expression brightened.

"Ezra! I'm so glad you're here. I need to get out of here before I knock my head against the wall," Stella said and looked at the old man as if saying that he was the reason why.

"I am still your father, and I have been in this business longer than you. You should listen to me," he complained.

Stella threw up her hands in defeat. "Do it then, but don't cry to me when it doesn't earn out."

Her father waved at her to leave. "Go and eat something, girl. It will help you think clearly and prove that I'm right."

Ezra couldn't help but smile at their interaction. Stella grabbed her handbag off a hook.

"Let's go, Ezra. I'm starving. How about you?" Stella said and led the way through a back entrance and into a narrow street.

"I used to argue with my father like that too," Ezra said with a soft laugh. "I think their stubbornness has something to do with the fact that they always will see us as children."

Stella nodded and hooked her arm through Ezra's as they walked through a small square and down a tight street. "Maybe Dom is right, and I should be focusing more on my magic than arguing with my father."

"Well, your husband is very handsome. I am sure that he could present a very convincing argument about the matter," Ezra replied with a smirk. Dom Aladoro was *gorgeous*. She was woman enough to admit that he could probably make her do whatever he wanted.

Stella snickered. "I'm sure he could, but he knows better than to try to tell me what to do."

"Handsome and wise. There aren't many of those around," Ezra said with a grin.

Stella opened the green door to a tiny restaurant with only five tables. There were photos and paintings on the walls of different time periods in Venice. A tall man wearing glasses gave them a friendly wave from behind a cash register and pointed to the table by the window.

"I've been coming here since I was a little girl. The food is my favorite in all of Venice." Stella looked across the table at Ezra. "Now, what brings you to my doorstep? Is everything okay with Zahir?"

"When I saw him this morning, he seemed fine." Ezra didn't know where to start. She needed advice from a woman, and Stella was the closest thing to a friend she had in Venice.

"Ah, I have a feeling this conversation is going to need wine." Stella went up to the counter and returned with two large glasses of red wine.

"We seem to only have wine conversations," Ezra said, accepting her glass.

Stella took a large sip and hummed. "Only conversations worth having, in my opinion. Why don't you just tell me that you slept with Zahir? Rip it off like a bandage, and then give me all the juicy details."

"Is it that obvious?" Ezra groaned.

Stella threw back her head and laughed. "You are positively glowing, my dear. Tell me, was it transcendental as it is rumored?"

"Most definitely. In my defense, I had a terrible day yesterday, and I really needed a pick-me-up."

Some of Stella's mirth disappeared. She reached across the table and put her hand on top of Ezra's and squeezed. "What happened? You can trust me, Ezra."

Ezra had a large mouthful of her wine and ended up telling Stella everything, including the vision she'd had when she touched the obsidian chip. She couldn't hide any details from her if she was going to ask for help.

Ezra's heart hurt as she thought of the colored roof of Zahir's ship and the years he'd spent as a slave. She wouldn't let Zahir be caught by the Cabal, even if it meant lying to him to keep him out of it. The golems would be the least of their problems if the Cabal weaponized Zahir.

Ezra wasn't one to give graphic details on her lover's prowess, but Stella was sneaky, and she had a few details that left Stella giggling. They ordered pasta, and Ezra presented Stella with her plan.

"I saw the mage this morning and gave him theoretical papers and formulas to back up what I told him," Ezra said and leaned her elbows on the table. "If my plan works, they will take me to the workshop tonight. I will be able to either destroy all the golems with a spell, or if that's too dangerous, I will give them another trick sigil to keep them happy. As soon as I am out of there, I will be able to lead Zahir to it."

Stella toyed with her wine glass. "Have you run this grand scheme by him at all?"

"No. I can't. He was talking about wrapping me up in a feather blanket and not letting me out of his sight again. I can't risk telling him because he will try to stop me," Ezra replied. She tried to ignore the squirming feeling inside of her. She didn't like lying to Zahir or potentially upsetting him.

"He is only trying to protect you. He cares about you. Anyone can see that," Stella replied.

"I don't want to hurt him, but I want these guys stopped. They will lead me right to them. You're a Raven. Would you pass up such an advantage?" Ezra asked.

"No, I wouldn't, but it's my job. Arkon has the Inquisitors arresting two of the Cabal members. Would it not be worth it to see what they say?"

Ezra shook her head. "No, because while they are being convinced to give up their Cabal's names, the rest of the members could be shipping the golems out and scattering. We will miss them, and I can't handle the thought."

"Is that why you are telling me all this? Do you need help?" Stella asked, giving in.

Ezra nodded. "Sort of. I need someone to know of my plans if anything should happen to me. The djinn that Zahir has watching over me might tail me if the mage comes for me, but I don't know what kind of warding they have up. It might stop them from being able to get close."

"Okay, well, how about this? I won't tell Zahir of this plan if you let me keep an eye on things. I can follow you to the work-shops and let Arkon and Zahir know where you are once you are inside. They will be able to close in on the place while you are distracting them," Stella replied. It was a good idea, and it would mean that Ezra was already in the workshop. She could try to disable the golems, and if all else failed, Stella would send in backup.

"Agreed." Ezra shook Stella's hand. "But no telling Zahir about this. He will interfere, and I can't have them hurting him."

"Can you blame him for wanting to protect you? He's besot-ted. It must be quite a scary thing for an immortal like him to care about a fragile little human," Stella said with a knowing smile.

"I'm trying to protect *him* right now. It's more important." Ezra's cheeks were hot, and she couldn't afford to entertain her growing feelings for him. "And I don't think he cares about me the way you are suggesting. We are friends at most, and we are still caught up in the magic of the bargain."

"Wow, you really can't accept the idea that he cares about you," Stella said with a shake of her head.

Ezra groaned. "Because it makes no sense. He's the fucking King of the Djinn! Why would he see me as anything but a distraction?"

"Because he was with you for a second time, and that's not something he ever does with lovers. He actually slept in the same bed with you, too. That doesn't sound like a mere distrac-tion to me," Stella replied, and a spark of jealousy shot through Ezra. She didn't want to think about Zahir being with anyone else. She kind of hated herself for feeling so possessive of someone that she could never be with.

"So what? It's not like I can have a real relationship with him," Ezra said, her temper flaring. "I doubt he's capable of fidelity, and I wouldn't be able to handle not having it. I'm too smart to fall for a fucking djinn."

"And I was too smart to fall for a shedu. Look how that turned out," Stella said, her green eyes sparkling with mischief.

"He's your mate. That changes everything. It's a bond that goes beyond station and normal attraction." Ezra drained her wine, feeling way too cynical for her own good. "My parents were like that. So in love with each other. It was like they shone with it. When my mother died, my father was completely unmoored. He lost his foundation. I vowed never to love anyone like that because I'm the most like him. If I relied on anyone to keep me steady and I lost them, I would go even crazier than he did." Ezra let out an awkward laugh, embarrassed she had said so much. Stella looked thoughtful and sad, and Ezra couldn't handle it.

"Look, I'll deal with whatever is happening between Zahir and me after the Cabal is stopped. One disaster at a time, yeah?"

"You're right. Just don't close up your heart to something that could be great," she said with the soft smile of someone who was in love already.

"Whatever you say, Raven," Ezra replied with a roll of her eyes. She needed Stella to drop it. It hurt too much to think about because the truth was, she *did* want something with Zahir. To love a djinn was like loving a star—absolutely pointless because you could never possess them. To hope for anything more was to court disaster, and she'd had enough of that in her life already.

Hope is like wishes. Both are likely to backfire and leave you worse than before, Ezra thought glumly. She would never have Zahir. Not in the way she really wanted. She would enjoy what time they had left and then bow out with as much grace as she could when it was over.

Even Ezra didn't believe that lie, but what choice did she have?

CHAPTER TWENTY-FIVE

*E*zra tapped her fingers against her journal, fighting temptation. She had been contemplating writing to Zahir all afternoon. She missed him and didn't know how to deal with the feeling. She didn't like hiding things from him either, but she knew he would try to stop her.

Maybe you should be stopped, the voice of reason tried to tell her. Using yourself as bait was never a good idea. It was just the only idea she had.

Ezra wasn't the type to let anyone swoop in and solve all of her problems for her, no matter how tempting it was. She had been in a melancholy mood since seeing Stella, and she didn't like the twinge of heartache that had crept in after their conversation.

Ezra didn't like many people, but she liked Zahir. Possibly more than liked if she felt like being honest with herself. She was comfortable with him like she hadn't been with any other lover. She couldn't love him. It was too impossible. Besides, she barely knew him.

You're smarter than this, Ezra, she scolded herself. *You can never belong in his world. You are not djinn.*

It didn't matter she liked the other djinn too. She didn't feel so out of place with the magic she kept locked up. It settled in their presence instead of being on guard like it was with the other human mages and sorcerers. None of it made any sense.

The only person she knew that had similar abilities to her had been her mother. Her gift wasn't as powerful as Ezra's, so she pushed her daughter hard. To get a simple 'well done' from her had made Ezra feel unstoppable. Ezra would never forget how Lucia shone with happiness whenever she used her magic. She would get a glow about her that made you unable to look away. Ezra never had that talent, but she loved magic more than anything.

Perhaps all of the magic and history he represented was the reason she was helplessly drawn to the Djinn King, no matter how disastrous it would be to her heart.

The afternoon sun was staining the sky the color of old blood when a heavy knock rattled her front door. Ezra took a look through the peephole and grabbed her satchel bag. The pale-haired mage was waiting for her and smiled like a snake when she opened the door.

"It would seem that your magic checks out. Zachariah has asked you to inspect the golems this evening," he replied. His blue eyes looked at her bag. "That's all you need?"

"Yes. I have my tools and papers ready to go," Ezra replied too brightly. She hated the idea of going anywhere with the creep. She took a deep breath and locked the front door before stepping out of the safety of her wards.

Something flashed in the corner of her eye, and Ezra spotted Stella in the restaurant across the square drinking espresso. It made Ezra feel a little better knowing that the Raven had her back. She saw the djinn at her jewelry store frown and take a step in her direction. Shit. She couldn't have her reporting back to Zahir.

"Lead the way... Sorry, I don't know your name," Ezra said.

"Vladek. You can call me Vlad," the mage replied, giving her a smile. Ezra followed him, her fingers sketching a sigil behind her back. It shot straight at the djinn, colliding with her chest in a small starburst.

That will keep her busy for a while.

Vladek was talking, and Ezra's attention quickly snapped back to him. "We got off on the wrong foot, and I'm sorry for that. I really was following orders," he said like it was a valid excuse for torturing her.

Ezra's skin crawled. She forced herself to reply. "I understand. I am being forced to go with you right now."

"The med-mages in Venice are second to none. I knew they would heal you in no time," he replied as they walked out of the square and into the narrow corridor of streets. Ezra contemplated pushing him into a canal, her back aching in memory of his 'orders.'

"Are you bound with slave bonds too?" she asked.

"I'm bound by something far worse than slave bonds." Vladek shook his head. "Honor and duty."

"I see," Ezra said and didn't ask further questions. She wanted to kill the mage in front of her, not to get to know him.

A short walk later, they crossed a canal bridge and walked down the Fondamenta Fornasa Vecia. Ezra didn't know what she expected for the Cabal of the Wise's secret hideout, but it wasn't a half boarded-up three story building with a salt stained boat shed attached to it. The bricks were bare and crumbling, and someone had spray painted a dick on the side of it.

"How glamorous," Ezra said, staring up at the building.

Vladek shrugged. "It's better to be invisible when you are about to become traitors and sell out your government."

"Have some experience with that, do you?" Ezra asked.

Vladek laughed. "No. I love my country. It's the Republic that breeds traitors."

The way he said 'the Republic' with such snide derision gave his origin away. If Ezra had to guess, she would say he was Varangian. It didn't seem right. She had never heard of any other Varangian mages except for the Wolf Mage. He had to have some big balls to come to Venice.

Ezra clutched onto the strap of her bag and looked around. She couldn't see Stella, but hoped she wasn't too far away. Vladek unlocked the padlock hanging on the door and pulled it open.

"Mind your step," he said and gestured for Ezra to enter. She swallowed hard and stared at the darkness.

One more night of being brave, and this could all be over, she told herself and stepped through the door. Inside smelled of warm, damp salt and musty rot. Vladek shut the door and switched on a naked bulb that hung from the ceiling. He passed her, brushing unnecessarily up against her shoulder, and she fought the urge to slap him away.

Ezra's jaw hurt from gritting her teeth. She knew she had the power to take on the cocky mage and walk away. The more he underestimated her, the better it would be.

Vladek led her through the house where someone had knocked down part of a wall to widen a room. Her skin burned as they crossed through protection wards. She could feel them in walls and under her feet. She wasn't sure whether it was to keep magic out of it or in.

Inside the room was a workshop with scarred benches, clay carving tools, and small wooden boxes set out neatly in rows. A large kiln was pushed up against a far wall along with another table set up with engraving tools.

Six golems stood against the wall like oversized toy soldiers in the dim light. They weren't as well formed as the one that Zachariah had brought to her house, but that didn't make them less effective.

"You can use the benches to set up, but I'd suggest getting

started or—" he stopped mid threat as a gray heron sailed through an open window and shifted into a rail thin man.

"Vladek! We have a problem," the shifter gasped, leaning over his knees to try to catch his breath.

"Well? Spit it out, man," Vladek snarled.

"Inquisitors were seen arresting Zachariah and Giuseppe an hour ago. They were pulled from their homes and taken to the palace." The shifter's eyes went to Ezra. "What the fuck is she doing here? We all need to leave the city! The Doge's sorcerers will—" The man's words choked off as Vladek slid a thin dagger into his throat. The shifter's eyes went wide as he sank to his knees and collapsed in a growing puddle of blood. Ezra bit down on the inside of her cheek to stop herself from screaming. The mage pulled the blade free and wiped it on the dead man's shirt.

"It looks as if our timeline has been moved up, *signorina*," he said calmly. "You had best get these golems working, for your own sake. Try not to get distracted, or you'll end up like him."

Ezra swallowed the bile creeping up her throat and pulled out different types of paper and colored inks. The mage was watching her closely, so she went over to the golems and ran her hands over the first one. She could feel the magic infused into the clay. She hated that the project that had brought Judah and her closer together was now forever going to be tainted with all that had happened since.

Ezra took a deep, calming breath and tried to steady her fear and emotions. She wouldn't let the vision she'd had of Zahir screaming in pain come to pass. She just needed to stay alive and co-operate long enough for Stella to send for the Inquisitors. It would be over before Zahir knew about it. He would be safe, and Ezra would be free. That's all that mattered. She knew that Stella wouldn't leave her hanging, so Ezra picked up a pen and got to work.

CHAPTER TWENTY-SIX

Zahir returned to Venice that afternoon to find a message waiting for him from Arkon. He unfolded and scanned the lines.

Two arrests have been successful. They are being held in the Doge's prison. Tea and torture at 5? – Arkon.

Zahir laughed and tucked the letter into his robe. He would clear this mess up with the Cabal so he could focus on more important things, like how flexible Ezra could be in the positions he had in mind.

Zahir ran his hands through his hair and tried to push away thoughts of her. At least he had some kind of answer for why he couldn't get enough of her. *Your consort.*

It would rattle every djinn in the Republic when he told them such a bond was possible. They had always scoffed at the shifters and how ridiculous they got over their mates. They acted little better than beasts. Zahir was now regretting every teasing remark he had sent in Domenico's direction. Ezra had him feeling like a lovesick idiot, and he barely knew her. She had turned him into an overprotective, possessive beast, and he wanted nothing more than to tear the Cabal to bloody shreds.

The cells underneath the Doge's palace were worn and ancient, with small doorways and narrow corridors. The marble on the floor was soft and bowed looking from the thousands of feet that had trampled it over the centuries.

Arkon was waiting for Zahir at the top of the stairs leading to the cells that had been made especially for mages. He looked more disheveled than usual, with smudges of ash on his face and on the cuffs of his sleeves.

Zahir rubbed at the ash on his cheek. "Big night, Grand Sorcerer?"

"Big night and a big day. I haven't actually been to sleep yet." Arkon looked him over. "Where have you been?"

"I went to see the old king." Zahir waved off his questioning gaze. "I'll tell you about it later. Have you learned anything from our guests yet?"

Arkon shook his head. "I haven't even laid eyes on them. I have been waiting for you. They were picked up less than an hour ago, and I've had more important things to do."

"Hopefully, they will be able to tell us about their strange mage friend who has been causing trouble in the city. Ezra said he had an accent that she didn't recognize."

Arkon rested his hand on Zahir's shoulder. "You can sit this one out if you need to. I know she means a lot to you."

"And that's the reason that I can't. They put slave bonds on *my* consort," Zahir hissed, his temper already flaring.

"Your consort?" Arkon demanded, eyebrows so high they got lost under his wild curls.

"I'll tell you later." It wasn't the place to discuss the revelation of djinn having mates.

"Looks like you'll be telling me a lot later." Arkon opened the cell door. "After you, old friend."

Zahir picked up the edge of his robes so they wouldn't touch the dirty marble ground and ducked into the narrow cell. The two Cabal members were chained to the walls with iron spell-marked manacles.

They both had the decency to look frightened at the appearance of the King of Wands. Their eyes went even wider when the Grand Sorcerer joined the party.

Zahir looked at the older man. "Zachariah, I assume?"

"Yes? What is this about? Why have we been brought here?" he replied and straightened his shoulders.

Zahir had to admire his confidence, but as he looked at them, all he could see was the bonds around Ezra's beautiful arms and her back torn to shreds. Confidence wasn't going to save him. There wasn't a god, djinn, or doge that could stop Zahir from ensuring this man was dog meat.

"We have it under good authority that you and your Cabal of the Wise are seeking to create golems to sell to the Varangians," Arkon said, leaning against the back wall and looking thoroughly bored.

Zachariah snorted. "What authority? Who has been telling you such lies?"

The other man, Giuseppe, had a fine sheen of sweat on his face. He didn't have the confidence of his master, which made him smarter than he looked.

Zahir moved to stand directly in front of Zachariah. "You should be very careful about the next words that come out of your mouth," he said softly. His power was feeling erratic, and it wanted to do such horrible things. "Now, where are the golems?"

"I don't have any golems," Zachariah replied stubbornly.

"Maybe not working ones, but they have definitely been sculpted, ready for animation. Isn't that right, Giuseppe?" Zahir turned on the other man.

"Y-You can't arrest me for sculpting what I like," he stammered.

Arkon chuckled from the shadows. "We can arrest you for whatever the fuck we like, boy. We are the Council of Ten."

Zahir crossed his arms. "All right, if you don't want to talk about the golems, let's talk about the murder of Judah Eliyahu and the slave bonds you put on Ezra. I have seen them with my own eyes, so try and deny it, and it won't end well for you."

"That bitch went to you?" Zachariah hissed in outrage and spat. "I should have known she would betray us. I never thought she would lower herself to spread her legs for a fucking abomination."

Zahir's vision went red as the sands he'd been born in. He heard Arkon saying something, but he was too far gone. He grabbed Zachariah's head with both hands, and his power tore into his mind. Zahir got flashes of memory—a man who must've been Judah showing Zachariah his marvels, Ezra screaming as the bonds fused to her flesh, a dark workroom filled with unseeing eyes, a man with pale hair and cold eyes speaking in Varangian, a golden ring carved with magic.

"Zahir! Stop!" Arkon shouted and pulled him away. Zahir snarled wordlessly at the sorcerer for pulling him free. Zachariah slumped on the floor. He started to laugh, a horrible bubbling laughter of madness.

"Torture me all you like, King of the Djinn," he spat. "You are already too late. Ezra is gone. The golems will have life, and the Varangians will wipe the djinn from the Republic forever." Blood bubbled out of his mouth and ears, and he slid sideways on the cell floor and passed out.

Zahir turned to the artist. Piss stained the front of the man's pants, and he was shaking, his eyes glued to Zachariah.

"You had better be more co-operative if you don't want to end up like him," Arkon said, getting in between Zahir and Giuseppe. He shot a warning look over his shoulder. It took all of Zahir's willpower to back off.

"You have five minutes, sorcerer," he growled.

"Look, boy, my friend here is very partial to Ezra, so tell me quickly where she is," Arkon said, drawing Giuseppe's attention to him.

"The mage, Vlad… Ah, Vladek is his full name. He went to Zachariah today and said that Ezra needed to be taken into the workshop to animate the golems. They sent for her right before we were arrested," Giuseppe babbled.

"This Vladek… He is Varangian, isn't he? Has a penchant for magical whips?" Zahir asked, his voice going deadly cold.

Giuseppe nodded. "Yes. He was sent by his master, Ingvar Hardrada, to see what the holdup was on the delivery. Please. I was brought into this just as an artist."

"But you knew what you were making," Arkon said.

"I didn't think they were serious! Once you're in the Cabal, there is no getting out."

Zahir moved, grabbed the man by his throat, and pinned him to the cell wall. "Where did they take Ezra? Address, now!"

Giuseppe sobbed and croaked out, "It's on the Fondamenta Fornasa Vecia. It's the building closest to the water. The quickest way into the workshop is through the gondola shed. The house is full of wards." He was starting to cry as he rattled off further instructions. "She's already going to be there, and if she gives them what they want, Vlad will kill her or, worse, take her back to Varangia to help him build more soldiers. I heard him talking to Zachariah about trading for her, getting her permanently out of Venice so they could work on the golems without the secrecy."

Arkon pulled Zahir away to the far corner of the cell. "Go to Ezra. I will stay here and try to find out more about this Varangian mage. I *told* you there was someone else in the empire doing magic for them. They have pushed this propaganda about the Wolf Mage. It could be a cover to hide the other magic users."

"I don't care about the bloody war, Arkon!" Zahir snapped, and magic shivered over his skin. "I'm going to get my fucking consort."

CHAPTER TWENTY-SEVEN

Zahir landed in the Square of the Ghetto Nuovo in a pillar of flame and rage. People cried out in surprise and scattered as he fought to pull back the fury of his magic. He didn't trust the artist's babbling and his claim that they were going to take Ezra. She would have alerted him with her notebook. He would have felt her in pain. He had to check things for himself.

Lira, the djinn he'd assigned to watch over Ezra, was sitting on the paving stones in front of her stall, staring at nothing and singing to herself in the early evening darkness.

"What the fuck are you doing?" Zahir demanded, striding over to her.

Lira grinned up at him. "Catching the pinkie butterflies, so they tell me all of their secrets. Ohhh, there's a red one." She waved her hands, about to reach for the invisible bug. Zahir grabbed her by the shoulders and gave her a firm stake.

"Focus, Lira! Where is Ezra?"

Lira's eyes were dazed. He let his power touch her. Ezra's magic hit him like a slap. She had enchanted his djinn. *Fuck.*

Zahir released her and walked to Ezra's house. The wards

welcomed him and unlocked the front door. She had built him into her security. His heart lurched dangerously.

"Ezra! Are you here?" he called, moving through the lower floors. He could smell her maddening scent of myrrh, like she had just stepped out of the room seconds beforehand. His magic reached out for her presence and felt nothing. The house was empty.

"Fuck. Fuck. Fuck." He whirled on his heel and almost collided with Lira.

"She went... Ah, this magic... She was following a tall blond man. He's been to the house before," she struggled to get out before she collapsed into giggles and ran out of the house. Ezra had really fucked her up.

Zahir shut the door on his way out and threw in an extra layer of protection over the house. He needed to focus and find her. Karsudan said they were connected beyond the bargain. He hadn't felt her distress so wherever she was, Ezra wasn't in any pain.

Zahir spoke an ancient incantation under his breath. It revealed magical trails in the air left behind by mages. It was a frustratingly pointless spell in places like Venice, where every second person held some magical ability. He knew the feel of Ezra's power and reached out for it. A starburst of bronze light was on the other side of the square.

"Ah, so this is where you were standing when you knocked Lira on her ass," he muttered under his breath. He was torn between being impressed with Ezra's skill and wanting to murder her for disobeying him. Stay home. Stay safe. How fucking hard was that?

If Vladek had come to fetch her, she might have had no choice. Zahir was going to murder that fucking mage and give Ezra his head on a silver platter. Now, that would be the perfect courting gift.

Zahir followed the magic, and his stomach clenched. He

knew every canal and *calle* in the Wands District, and with every step, he was getting closer to the Fondamenta Fornasa Vecia.

The artist had been telling the truth. Miracles did happen.

Zahir turned onto the street, and a bolt of electricity shot through the darkness and collided with his shoulder.

"What the fuck!" he snarled. He looked up to where the attack had come from. A hooded figure gave him a cheeky wave from a nearby rooftop. Zahir hissed in frustration and teleported himself beside them and knocked the figure to their ass.

"Jesus, Zahir! It's me!" Stella said, pulling back her hood. "What the hell?"

"You attacked me! What was I supposed to do?" he replied.

"I gave you a little zap to get your attention. How many fulmian mages do you know, asshole?" Stella huffed and held out her hand. "Well? Help me up."

Zahir lifted her back to her feet. "Would you mind explaining to me what the hell you are doing up here?"

"I will if you don't get mad," Stella said.

"I am already mad, woman." Zahir's eyes narrowed. "If you don't tell me this minute, I will inform Domenico that you have been stalking rogue Varangian mages without him knowing."

Stella put her hands on her hips. "You are such a bitch when you want to be. I'm actually up here at the behest of your current *paramour*."

Zahir hadn't been expecting that. "Explain and be quick about it."

"She came and saw me today. She had a vision and was freaked out about it," Stella began. Zahir grew more pissed off and worried with each word out of her mouth. Ezra had a vision when she had touched the obsidian chips and had lied to him about it. The lying part hurt more than the sneaking around with Stella.

"Don't be mad, Zahir. She is genuinely trying to protect you in this situation. She loves you, even if she won't admit it yet.

She wouldn't risk her own safety like this if she didn't," Stella tried to console him. He was not in a consoling mood.

"She's my mate," Zahir admitted, feeling like he'd been knifed in the chest.

Stella's eyes went wide. "What? That's not…a thing for djinn."

"Apparently, it is. We don't use that word. We use consort, but it amounts to the same thing. Maybe you can understand why I'm so fucking mad at the both of you right now," Zahir said, pushing his hands through his hair. "You should have messaged me straight away when she came to you with this idiotic idea."

"Hey, don't put this on me. She has no idea she's your consort, does she?"

"Of course not! I didn't even know until this morning! I haven't seen her since."

Stella placed a hand on his arm. "For the record, she's lovely and very much her own woman. It wasn't a dumb idea, and she made sure she had me backing her up. She wanted to be taken so we could find out where they were keeping the golems. She was worried they were making rings or vessels to trap djinn. She was scared for you, but she was thinking clearly."

"So what have you been doing while she's trapped in that damn house?" Zahir demanded.

"I've been waiting to hear back from Arkon. I sent him a message to send the Inquisitors almost an hour ago," she said, a frown forming between her brows. "He hasn't gotten back to me."

Zahir cursed. "I know why. He's too busy in the Doge's prison, interrogating the other Cabal members about the fucking Varangian mage."

"He's in the house with Ezra," Stella replied.

"What? You've got to be fucking kidding me."

"No. He was sent to collect her. I saw a heron shifter go in there too about thirty minutes ago, but he hasn't come out again," she replied, biting her lip.

"Call Dom, Stella. He was meeting with Gio and Nico today. He might still be at the palace. Get him to find Arkon and send the fucking Inquisitors," Zahir replied. He wanted to level the building. He was so mad.

Stella was wise enough not to argue with him about it. "What are you going to do?"

"What do you think? I'm going to get my consort," Zahir snapped, his magic flaring along his arms. "And when she is safe, I'm going to throttle her for being so disobedient and making me fucking worry this much."

"Sure you will." Stella fought back a smile. "Good luck. Be ready for us when you see us. And don't kill anyone! Doge's justice and all that. Hey, baby," she said, brightening when Dom answered his phone. "So I've fucked up and need you to find Arkon. Zahir is about to do something dumb. Yes, more so than usual."

The fuck he was. Zahir flipped her off in annoyance. Going after Ezra was the smartest thing he would ever do. He didn't give a damn about anyone's justice but his own that night.

Zahir stepped off the side of the building, disappearing into the ether. He could feel Ezra's magic being worked, its song calling out to his own. He didn't think. He dropped through the building's chimney and rematerialized in the center of a workshop.

"Hello, sparrow. Fancy finding you here," he growled.

Ezra leaped up from a chair with a shout of warning. "Go, Zahir! Get out of here!"

Zahir froze as lines of complex warding shot into silvery life, like a magical net around him. He was caught like a fly in a fucking web. A deep voice started to laugh, and Zahir whirled. The mage was tall with silvery blonde hair and pale blue eyes.

"Let me guess, Vladek the Varangian?" he asked, forcing

down his sudden panic. Arkon and his Inquisitors wouldn't be far away. He would never live it down that the mighty Djinn King had got himself caught by a bunch of fucking human mages.

"Very good. You must be Zahir the Eternal," he said, his accent as thick as Ezra claimed. "I thought one as old as you would've been smarter."

"What can I say? I was blinded by love," Zahir replied, looking at Ezra. She only rolled her eyes.

"Idiot," she muttered, but she was smiling as she said it.

"You can't talk. You were the one who thought all of this..." Zahir gestured around him, "was a good idea. You and Stella are forbidden from being friends from here on out."

"And you're going to stop me? You've just walked straight into a trap! The very thing I was trying to prevent!" Ezra exclaimed.

Sweet Creator, spare him. She was beautiful when she got angry. Zahir forgot all about his situation and just grinned at her like an idiot. She grinned back.

Vladek looked between them and started to laugh. "Well, isn't this interesting? Let's see how fast Ezra works now that she has proper motivation."

White searing pain burned through Zahir, and he screamed before he could hold it back. Needles of pain electrified his entire body, and he collapsed onto the floor. Ezra was shouting, her fists beating against the warding.

"Leave him alone!" she begged, tears tracking down her face.

Zahir shook his head. "Don't do it, sparrow." Like always, his beautiful Ezra ignored him.

"Please," she begged Vladek. "I'll do it. I'll give you the sigil. Just don't hurt him anymore."

CHAPTER TWENTY-EIGHT

*E*zra's hands were shaking as she pulled out a fresh piece of paper. She tried not to look at Zahir because she would get scared and panicked again. She couldn't believe he had gotten himself caught in the wards. Where was Stella? She was meant to stop him from doing anything stupid.

"How has your day been, sparrow?" Zahir asked. He was sitting cross-legged in the center of the wards and was looking bored.

"Really? You want to chat?" she said irritably.

"There is nothing else to do. You aren't really going to give this clown the power to animate these golems, are you?" he replied. He kept his tone light, but his dark eyes were intense.

"I don't really have a choice now, do I?" Ezra looked over the workshop to where Vladek was sitting in a battered armchair.

Vladek had a blank smile on his face. "No, you don't. Not unless you want to end up like him." He had left the heron shifter on the floor in his own blood. Vladek didn't seem to be worried about the warning Zahir had tried to give to him. Ezra wondered what made him so confident in his abilities to get away from the Republic unscathed.

Zahir's expression was merciless. "You know there is no way you're going to walk away from here alive. It would be better if you let me and Ezra go. It might make me feel less inclined to tear your skin off, piece by piece."

"You are in no position to be making threats, djinn. You will be my slave before the night is out. If Ezra doesn't hurry up, I will make you do horrible things to her once you are under my control," Vladek replied with a soft chuckle.

He can't have Judah's sigil, can he? Ezra fought to keep the panic off her face. She thought she felt a slight tingle of Zahir's magic reaching for her. Maybe if she tried to hold out...

Zahir writhed as the surrounding wards triggered. Vladek smiled as he watched him fight to stop from screaming.

"Please, stop. I'm working on them as fast as I can!" Ezra shouted.

"You are fucking about, trying to waste my time, and I can't have it. Make this golem work, or I'll fucking kill your lover," Vladek snarled back. The wards went silent, and Zahir told him to go fuck a pig in Italian.

Ezra shut them out and started to sketch the first *shem*. She didn't have time to create another fake, so she modified the one that she had first given to Zachariah. She drew another and another until she had one for each of the clay figures. They just had to move long enough for Stella to arrive.

Ezra rolled up the tiny scroll and approached the first golem. She touched her fingers to its cold clay lips and sent a spark of her magic through it. The golem opened its mouth, and Ezra placed the scroll inside of it. Magic danced over its clay body, and it shuddered to life, its eyes glowing bright as they became alert.

Vladek came to inspect the creature. He asked, "How does it know to obey me?"

"Place your fingers on his lips and send the essence of your magic through it," Ezra replied.

Vladek did as she instructed, and the golem rumbled, "Master."

"Stand on one leg," the mage demanded, and the golem did so. He laughed and pointed. "Now, do the others, girl."

"Ezra, please stop this," Zahir begged.

"I can't. I won't be responsible for your death. I can't lose anyone else I care about," she said, blinking back her tears. She sent up another prayer to any god that would listen that Stella would hurry the hell up. She moved through each golem until they were all alive and staring patiently at Vladek.

"It's done. Please, I did what you asked," Ezra said to Vladek.

"Hold her," he commanded. Ezra tried to run, but the golem grabbed her by the back of her shirt and lifted her off her feet. Zahir went crazy, bashing against the warding and shouting for her.

"You didn't really think I would honor the Cabal's promise to you? I serve my master, just like you will. A mage that creates wonders can't be used to make such things for the Republic," Vladek said.

"You fucking bastard," Ezra snarled and kicked. Her hand started to sketch an attack sigil in the air.

"Oh, no, none of that," Vladek said, grabbing her hands. Cold power froze her, and Ezra screamed as her fingers broke. Blackness and shock dragged her under, and the last thing she heard was Zahir screaming for her.

* * *

EZRA DIDN'T KNOW how long she was out, but when she came back around, it was to the realization that she was hanging from something. She opened her eyes and tried to stand. Her feet were just touching the dirty floor. She was hanging from the roof, her hands broken and numb.

No, no, no. Her vision had come true when she had done everything she could to prevent it.

Vladek's pale face appeared in front of her. "Ezra? You will want to be awake for this," he said and tapped her face. Ezra kicked out at him, narrowly missing and making the horrible mage laugh. He held up a golden ring with an oval face. Carved in dark lines on the face was Judah's sigil.

"Does this look familiar? Your papa made it. He said that it would be powerful enough to trap a djinn. What do you think?" he asked her.

Ezra shook her head, trying to think straight through the pain. "Don't count on it. He gave the Cabal fake *shem* designs after all."

"Let's try it out. I have time to kill while I wait for my ride, and I would love an enslaved djinn to take home to Kyiv," Vladek replied.

"No, leave him alone. Please, I'll willingly go with you, but leave him be," Ezra begged. She pulled at the chains holding her upright. She couldn't handle the thought of her djinn being enslaved again, trapped and bound to some psychopath.

Zahir didn't look afraid. He looked tired, like he had seen a hundred overambitious, power-hungry bastards like the one in front of him. "Believe me, boy, you don't want to go down this road. It won't end well for you. It never does."

"Be quiet, slave. I'm not interested in your warnings," Vladek snapped. He had drawn complex runes around Zahir in a circle, joined to a smaller circle in a twisting line. He placed the ring in it and stepped back. He started to chant, and the runes lit up one at a time. Zahir's calm demeanor shifted, and he went wild, shifting out of his human form to flame and shadow as he fought against the magic tying him down.

Ezra sobbed and tried to move her fingers to create some spark of magic to disrupt Vladek's spell, but they refused to work.

When you can do nothing else, you dance, her father's voice whispered to her. *Dance.*

Ezra took a centering breath and summoned her magic. Instead of directing it to her hands, she forced it to her feet. She knew from her studies that in some cultures, magic spells were channeled through the sacred steps of a dance. She had to try something. She couldn't let Zahir be a slave again.

Ezra shut her eyes and focused on the wild violin music Judah had loved. She let the memory overtake her, and her feet began to move of their own accord. Tears tracked down her cheeks as she danced her sigil, pouring all of her magic and feelings for her impossible Djinn King into it. She danced the day they first met on the boat, the way he'd kissed her on the dance floor and made her laugh in the rooftop garden. She danced their laughter in the darkness and the feel of his magic against hers, the way he made her feel safe enough to fall asleep in his arms.

Ezra gasped as hot sizzling power scorched her veins, and her entire body blazed with magic. It filled her up, building and building, until she could barely contain it. She fixed her eyes on the golem closest to her, and the magic shot out of her with a thought. It struck the golem in its chest before the power jumped, pouring into the other creatures, igniting them one at a time and burning away the traces of Vladek's cold magic in them.

Vladek had his back to her and was lost in his own magic, drawn deep in the binding spell. Zahir was staring at her, his shadow and flame body doing nothing to hide his awe. He was elemental and beautiful. She could feel his magic trying to reach out for her. It was a power she knew that was written on her bones and made just for her.

"Mine," she said, her voice deep and distant.

Zahir placed his hands on the wards and mouthed. "Yes."

Ezra swung to face the golem closest to her. "Stop the mage, but don't kill him," she commanded.

The golem swung out at an unsuspecting Vladek, its clay palm coming down hard on his outstretched forearm. He screeched as it broke, his cold magic dispersing in a cloud. The golem kicked, breaking Vladek's leg and sending him toppling to the ground.

"Hold him," Ezra said, and the golem pinned the sobbing, swearing mage to the floor, his clay hand holding him by the back of his neck.

The door to the workshop blew open and a furious Arkon charged in, magic crackling and ready to unleash. He looked at Zahir, a still glowing Ezra, and the crying Varangian mage.

"Too late again, asshole," Zahir said.

"Caught by a mage's web. You're a fool of a djinn," the sorcerer replied and tore the wards to shreds. Zahir stumbled back into his human form before hurrying to Ezra.

"I have you, sparrow," he said, his magic dissolving the chains that held her up. He caught her as she fell forward.

"You have to get the ring," she whispered, her hands throbbing. Arkon was already poking around the mage on the floor like he was an interesting bug the sorcerer was contemplating pinning to a board.

"You have to be healed first," Zahir replied softly. He sent his power through her, mending the bones of her fingers. Ezra smothered her cries into his shoulder until the pain vanished.

"Y-You have to get the ring," she repeated.

Zahir set her down. "I can't touch it. You can though."

Ezra stumbled over to the smaller circle, disabled the surrounding runes, and picked up the heavy golden ring. It thrummed with power. Magic flared, and she felt the spell tethered to Zahir. The ring burned before sliding itself onto her index finger and sticking there like glue.

"What the fuck?" She whirled around to ask Zahir what had just happened, but the words died in her throat. The Djinn King smiled mysteriously and slowly lifted a finger to his lips.

The spell had worked, and he was now bound...to her.

CHAPTER TWENTY-NINE

*Z*ahir felt like he'd been wrapped inside a carpet and run over by a stampede of horses. He wanted nothing more than to sink into a hot bath with Ezra perched on his lap. His duties and sorting out the traitors had to come first.

"What did you do to him?" Arkon asked, poking the mage on the floor with the toe of his boot.

"I used the golem to shatter his arm and leg. I think he's passed out," Ezra replied. She was rubbing her hands together like she was trying to warm them. Her poor beautiful hands. Zahir didn't know how she had the strength to use magic without them. He needed to know everything, but he didn't dare ask with Arkon there. He was too curious, and the last thing he wanted was the sorcerer trying to recruit her for his Ravens.

"Alright, Ezra, please remove your golem. I have a lovely cell waiting for this man," Arkon instructed.

"Don't tell her what to do," Zahir grumbled.

Ezra's power flashed like a hot touch, sizzling the air as she approached the golem. She placed a hand on the clay man's shoulder. "Release him and move back, please."

The creature obeyed, and Arkon raised a brow at Zahir. He knew what the sorcerer was thinking. *Clay soldiers could be useful.* Zahir shook his head, and Arkon threw up his hands in a huff.

Ezra saw the exchange and knew without asking what was going on. She touched the golem's lips and pulled the *shem* free.

"I'm sorry, but none of these golems will leave here," she said to Arkon. She removed the scrolls one at a time before placing them in Zahir's hands. "Burn them for me."

"With pleasure, my sparrow," Zahir replied and turned them to ash. "Arkon, make yourself useful and get the slave bonds off Ezra."

"I thought you knew how to remove them! That's why I made the bargain with you," Ezra demanded, eyes narrowing.

Arkon chuckled. "He was going to kill Zachariah. When a mage dies, his spells do too."

"Guilty as charged. I still want to kill him, but I'm unwilling to let you be bound to him a second longer," Zahir replied, crossing his arms.

Ezra sighed and held out her arms to Arkon. "Is he always like this?"

"Only when it comes to you," Arkon replied with a sly wink. "Now, why don't you tell me why you were glowing like a sun when I walked in?"

Ezra's skin tingled as Arkon placed his hands over her wrists. "I danced out a sigil to take control of the golems, and it pulled out a lot more magic out of me than I thought."

"Magic out of you? That's not what I felt," Arkon mused, and the slave bonds rose to the surface of her skin.

Zahir kicked Arkon in the back of the heel. "Focus on the task at hand, sorcerer. You can talk about magic later."

He didn't want Arkon scaring Ezra when she'd already had the night from hell. He would get her fed, rested, and well sexed before broaching the subject that she was his consort and had somehow channeled part of his power. He didn't want to lose her over it. He almost had that night due to his own stupidity, and he hated it.

"Zahir? Are you okay?" Ezra asked, her brow furrowing. She had felt his turmoil. Fuck.

"No, but I will be," he replied. They both would be. He'd make sure of it.

Ezra looked about to press the matter when a blonde head appeared through the workshop door with a group of Inquisitors.

"There you three are! Oh, four," Stella said, spotting Vladek on the ground. Arkon had placed magical nulling cuffs on his wrists in case he woke up and decided to be brave.

"What took you so long?" Zahir demanded. He looked at the Inquisitors. "I need you to guard this place until all the other Cabal members are arrested."

Arkon looked up from Ezra's wrists. "I got the names out of Giuseppe the Talker. I've already sent men to take care of it," he replied before Stella could.

Stella wrapped an arm around Ezra. "Are you okay? Arkon, stay focused. We need to take Ezra home."

"No, Ezra is coming with me," Zahir replied stubbornly.

"Am I?" she asked. Her lips twitching in amusement. *How* she could be amused after such a horrible night was beyond him.

A roar shook the street outside, and Zahir smirked at Stella. "You're in trouble now."

Domenico Aladoro came through the back entrance of the old house and into the workroom. His eyes were glowing, ready for a fight and finding it all over. Ezra let out a small squeak as she took him in with wide eyes.

"Oh, don't let him bother you. Dom's a pussycat," Arkon told her.

Dom let out a warning growl. "You and I are going to have a

serious conversation about the danger you keep putting my wife in, sorcerer."

"Really?" Arkon said with an amused glint in his eyes. "Because this debacle was *her* idea, Domenico. It went to shit because she didn't tell me what was happening."

"I tried to, but you didn't read your messages!" Stella retorted, hands on her hips.

"I never read my messages! You know this about me!"

"Enough, the pair of you," Dom snarled. He touched Stella's cheek lightly. "Are you okay?"

"I'm fine. I was late too," she said. She stood up on tiptoes and kissed his cheek. "Ezra saved the day."

"Hi," Ezra greeted. Her voice was a little too breathy for Zahir's liking.

"It's nice to meet you. I wish it was under different circumstances," Dom replied, turning on a charming smile that had Ezra's cheeks flaring red.

"Now, now, none of that Dom. Don't distract Arkon from his work," Zahir said, stepping in between them. "You should have a look at that over there. You know, before I kill him."

Dom kneeled beside the unconscious mage. "How in God's name did a Varangian get smuggled into the city? Nico is going to be so pissed off."

"We don't know yet, but if anyone can figure out how to do it, Nico will. I'll schedule him in to chat to the mage after we get him in Gio's dungeon," Arkon said, not looking up from whatever he was doing on Ezra's arms.

"You had better. Although, I don't envy the mage. Nico is wound up so tight, he'll probably beat the shit out of him if you don't watch him," Dom replied, standing once more.

Zahir laughed. "I might pull up a chair and let him loose for my entertainment."

"That's a pretty ring you have. Where did you get it?" Stella asked Ezra, drawing Zahir's attention back to them.

"Just something I found amongst my father's things. I wanted to wear it because I missed him," Ezra replied.

She was smart, his consort. Zahir could feel the invisible manacles chaining him to the trinket. That was one more thing they would have to deal with.

"Your family sounds like interesting people," Arkon said, and his magic sizzled in the air. Ezra gasped as the manacles fell off her arms and vanished into nothing. She rubbed at her wrists before a gorgeous smile broke over her face, and she launched herself at Arkon.

"Thank you! Thank you!" she said, hugging him around his neck and kissing both of his cheeks. Because he couldn't help being a prick, Arkon cuddled her back and winked at Zahir over the top of her head.

"You're most welcome, Ezra," he said, giving her his most charming smile. "You know, I'm very fascinated by your magical abilities, perhaps after—"

Zahir couldn't take it a second longer. "One more word, sorcerer, and I swear to the Creator, I will teleport you straight to the ass end of Varangia."

"Zahir! You can't talk to the Grand Sorcerer like that," Ezra gasped.

"The fuck I can't," he grumbled. "I know him, and if you're not careful, you'll be recruited into his little web of intrigue in no time."

"I can't believe you think I would do such a thing," Arkon said, aghast.

"You would," Stella, Dom, and Zahir replied at the same time.

Ezra laughed at them all, and something eased a little in Zahir's chest. He held out a hand to her, and she took it, letting him draw her close.

"Have you got this under control, Arkon?" Zahir asked him.

The sorcerer was wise enough to nod. "Go on. I'll message you to let you know when the rest of the Cabal is secure. Ezra?

I'm going to need you to come in for some questioning and a statement about everything."

"Whatever you need to keep them locked up," she replied with a vicious smile.

"*After* she has time to rest, Arkon," Zahir added.

Arkon put his hands on his hips. "Justice doesn't sleep, Zahir."

"But we do." Zahir pointed at the still unconscious Vladek. "Don't you have a new Varangian mage to question about your girlfriend?"

"Kindly fuck off," Arkon replied half-heartedly, though none of them missed the way his eyes glowed in anticipation. If he could prove his theory about Varangia having other mages... Zahir didn't want to think about it.

Ezra wrapped her arms around him. "Take us home?" she whispered.

"Of course, my sparrow," he replied, and they disappeared in a cloud of bronze.

CHAPTER THIRTY

*E*zra blinked, and they were out of the filthy, dilapidated building and back on Zahir's boat. It wasn't the home she thought he would take her to.

"What's wrong?" he asked.

"I thought you would take me back to my home," she admitted, trying to fight the feelings that were suddenly attacking her. "The Cabal is caught. The slave bonds are gone." Even the last tally mark was gone. Clearly, the magic thought that a night of terror and torture still counted as a night together. Seeing her blank skin sent irrational panic through her.

"And what? You thought I was going to dump you in an empty house after everything that's happened?" he asked, his brows drawing together. He was pissed.

Ezra stepped back from him. "I don't know, Zahir. Maybe?"

"You'll be lucky if I ever let you out of my sight again," he growled, closing in on her. Ezra bumped against the bathroom door. Zahir caged her in. "Do you have any idea how insane it was to use yourself as bait? I almost lost my damn mind when Stella told me."

Ezra's heart was in her throat, but she wasn't going to let

him intimidate her. "It got us what we needed, didn't it? The Varangian mage is caught, and the Cabal is stopped."

"I don't give a fuck about them! I care about you, and you could have gotten yourself killed," he said. His hands rested on her cheeks. "Don't ever do something so reckless again. My heart can't take it."

"Zahir, I…" Ezra didn't know what to say. Her own heart was beating too fast. She touched the ring on her finger. The ring. "Shit. I'll get this thing off, I promise. I will free you from it and me as soon as possible. You can go back to being the king and everything will be fine."

"I don't *want* to be free from you," he said, his eyes flicking in frustration. "It's never been about the bargain, and it's certainly not about the ring. It's about you and me. It has always been. I want you, always. Why can't you understand that?"

Ezra's chest ached. How could she trust this feeling? "You can't be serious, Zahir. You're the *King* of the Djinn! I'm a human, and not a remarkable one at that."

"You're wrong," he replied, his eyes dancing with magic. His lips brushed against hers. "You're my consort, and I will have you, Ezra. I don't care how long it takes me to convince you that it's true."

"Y-Your consort? What are you *talking* about?" she demanded.

Zahir just grinned at her, like he couldn't help it. "Come for a bath with me, and I'll tell you all about it."

Ezra's eyes narrowed. "Are you serious?"

"Deadly. We both smell like a bad night, and I want to have a bath," he said, moving her away from the door and going into the bathroom. He stripped off his shirt, his grin widening when he saw her staring. "Come on. Have a bath with me, Ezra."

It was so rare for him to use her real name that she found herself toeing off her boots. She really couldn't resist him. Zahir's magic danced around the bathroom, lighting candles and turning on the bath taps until everything was steaming and golden.

Zahir sank into the bath, stroking the top of the water with a finger as he watched her undress. She was shaking a little and didn't know why. This night had taken so many twists that she didn't know if she could handle another. Zahir held out his hand and helped her into the tub. She purposely settled in the opposite end of the bath.

"What are you doing all the way over there, sparrow?" he asked with a playful smile.

"You said you would tell me everything if I had a bath with you. Well?" she demanded, sounding far braver than what she felt. She wanted nothing more than to sit in his lap to make her forget she'd ever heard of the damn Cabal of the Wise.

Zahir leaned back with a sigh, his muscular brown arms coming to rest on either side of the tub, hot water dripping over his shoulders and chest. God, he was beautiful. Ezra's self-control wavered.

"Stop it," she growled.

Zahir laughed, a sound like sin. "Stop what? I haven't even started. Come here, you are too far away from me."

"Zahir. Just tell me," Ezra said, refusing to budge.

"I went to see the old king, Karsudan, this morning," he replied, his playful expression sobering. "God, this day has been long."

"The old king? I didn't know there was one before you," she said, her curiosity getting the better of her.

"I took over at his behest when the Republic was forming once more," Zahir replied. His hand found her foot and began to massage it gently. "He is one of the oldest of my kind, and I needed his advice regarding you and how our magic reacts to each other. More than that, how *I* react to you."

"How do you react to me?" she whispered, eyes wide. This was not where she expected the conversation to go.

"I want you, all of you, all of the time," Zahir said, his grip on her ankle tightening. "My magic was erratic from the moment this foot touched the deck of my boat. It was all a sign of something that I didn't believe was possible."

Ezra flicked some water at him. "You're speaking in riddles again."

"No, I'm not. I'm trying to tell you this in the right way because you want to argue with me about everything."

"I do not," she said and then laughed at his expression.

"Too far away," he muttered and pulled her leg. They met halfway, water splashing over the sides as her legs went around him. Her arms circled his neck, and she knew he'd won.

"Hey, that was cheating," she complained, gently flicking the small golden hoops in his ears. She never could resist him for long. Zahir picked up a small purple soap and washed down her back in calming strokes.

"You are my consort, Ezra. Karsudan confirmed it," he continued, resting his forehead against hers.

"Consort. What does that even mean, Zahir?"

"It means, when the Creator made djinn, it made us as a pair. That our magic would be able to be shared with another. You are my missing half," he replied, his eyes burning into hers.

Ezra shook her head. "That's not possible. I'm not a djinn. How can I share your power?"

"Karsudan said that you will have a djinn in your bloodline. Your power is in creation, so is ours. But more than that, you used my magic already," he said, lifting her hand that held the golden ring. "At the warehouse when you danced, I could barely breathe. You were elemental. Glorious. I've never seen anything so beautiful. You drew on my magic. I don't know how, but you did. I felt it, and you wielded it as easily as your own. Why do you think Arkon found it so amusing? He could feel my magic being used by you."

Ezra's heart swelled dangerously. It was impossible. It had to be. She stared at her hands and then back up at him. "But I'm human. I can never... *We* can never..."

"There is a ceremony, like a djinn wedding, that would bind us, and you would share in my immortality. Karsudan said that he would do it." He kissed her hand. "I already have one ring on your finger binding us. What's one more?"

"But I'm going to be able to break the sigil on this!" she complained.

Zahir kissed away her other protests. "I'm not saying we need to do the ceremony tomorrow, my love. I know you're going to need some time to process things and wait to see if what I say is true. I can wait. I just don't want you to run from me. From us."

Ezra rubbed at her face. "But you're djinn. Being monogamous isn't a concept for you guys."

"Not true. I've always been faithful to my lovers. You need to stop listening to rumors. Also, how could I ever want anyone else when I have my consort?" Zahir argued, pulling her closer. "I know you are scared to trust me, but believe me, Ezra, I've had thousands of lovers over the years. I don't need any more of them. I just need my consort. I want you."

Ezra smiled, and she felt it fill her entire being. "You do?"

"If you'll have me," he replied, stroking her cheeks.

"Can I think about it?" she teased.

His eyes flared. "You have to? I can't believe—"

Ezra kissed him, unable to torment him for long. It was like lighting an inferno. Ezra's hands buried in his dark hair, mouth burning against his. Her whole body wanted to claim him. Zahir groaned, dragging her up against him so her breasts pressed against his chest. His dick was already hard, and Ezra dropped a hand so she could stroke him and toy with his piercing.

"Fuck, Ezra," he gasped, and she loved that she could make him sound that way. His hand grabbed hers and pulled her away. "I need to get into a bed right this second."

"I thought you wanted to have a bath," she said and rubbed herself against him.

Zahir's hair was sticking up riotously from her hands, making him look wilder and more wicked than usual. "And now I want to fuck you."

Zahir stood up, carrying her with him as he got out of the tub. She was laughing as he dried her roughly with a towel, refusing to let her go the entire time. He carried her into the main room and lay back on the bed, taking her with him so she was on top of him. The room filled with candles on every surface, making the world glow golden.

"This is much better," he said, putting his hands behind his head. Ezra leaned down and kissed him, her tongue flicking against his. She gasped when another set of hands stroked down her back, and an invisible mouth kissed her neck.

"You and your tricks," she teased softly.

Zahir leaned up onto his elbows. "I love you, and one set of hands on you isn't enough for me," he replied, shifting so he could nip his way down her neck.

Ezra cupped his face in her shaking hands. "I love you too," she said and kissed his happy smile.

Zahir rolled her onto her back, caressing and kissing down her chest. Flushed red marks appeared where he kissed and sucked at her breasts before spreading her legs and teasing her clit with his pierced tongue until she was gasping for breath.

"I think I'm going to keep you like this until you agree to be my consort," Zahir said, brushing his beard up against her sensitive inner thigh.

"I make better decisions when there is a dick inside of me, I swear," she retorted, trying to hide the tremble in her legs.

Zahir chuckled and lifted her hips up off the bed. "You really are perfect for me," he said, and thrust deeply into her. Ezra's back arched, her hands gripping the sheets, trying to find purchase. "That's better, isn't it, my consort?" Zahir circled his hips, moving inside of her slow and deep.

"Yes, fuck. More," she begged. She would never get enough of him, of them being and moving as one. Ezra still couldn't believe that she could have him permanently. But she wanted to. Zahir's eyes sparkled with magic above her as he thrust deeper and faster into her.

Ezra pulled him down to kiss him breathlessly. "I love you," she whispered. Zahir's eyes went full bronze, and she was suddenly floating up from the bed. She cried out at the impossible change in positions.

"Don't worry. I won't drop you, my love," Zahir said.

She hung onto him, her nails scoring his thighs. She could feel her orgasm starting to rattle her, and she cried out with each hard thrust of his dick.

One of Zahir's hands went around the side of her neck, and he pushed up against her for a dirty kiss. "Tell me you're mine, Ezra."

"Please, please, I'm so close," she babbled.

"Tell me you're mine, and I'll let you come," he growled against her lips.

"Fuck, I'm yours, Zahir. I'm yours."

His smile turned filthy. "Promise?"

"Zahir!" she snapped, making him laugh.

"Good girl." He kissed her deeply. "I'm yours too, Ezra. Don't forget it."

Ezra's hands fell helplessly in the air around them as he pulled her legs over his shoulders and resumed fucking the life out of her. An invisible mouth started to suck hard on her clit, and she couldn't hold herself back any longer. Her magic and orgasm roared through her, and she exploded like a supernova. She was glowing like a sun, and Zahir... He was smiling like she was the best thing he had ever seen in his long, long life.

CHAPTER THIRTY-ONE

*Z*ahir was struggling his way through a council meeting a week later with as much grace as he could muster. Which was none at all. He didn't want to leave Ezra's arms for another month, but Arkon and Gio's incessant messages over the past five days had gotten too much for him.

While they had been tracking down the Cabal, the Wolf Mage had committed another atrocity. The Republic's men had been ambushed in the dead of night by monstrous creatures, leaving only fleshy pulp and bone behind.

"It wasn't her," Arkon argued, his cheeks red with frustration.

"Who else was it then? Until we have a definite answer to that question, the deaths are laid at her feet," General Josefina Serpente D'Argento replied, her tone icy.

"We have another Varangian mage under our feet in the dungeon at this very minute. Varangia is clearly branching out in its recruitment," Arkon snapped. "We rule the seas, and perhaps that's why they are trying to attack our land troops with any means they have."

"What I want to know," Nico interrupted in his calm, deep voice, "is how that bastard got through our patrols and into our city to begin with. If there is a gap in our defenses, however small, it must be plugged up."

"You can come to the dungeons with me after the meeting, and we can poke him with something sharp until he tells us," Zahir told him. He looked at Gio. "Is that all for today?"

The Doge's eyes narrowed. "No."

Zahir was contemplating leaving a copy of himself in the chair and disappearing when a red-faced messenger came in. "Apologies for interrupting, but I have an urgent message for General D'Argento."

"Out with it," Josefina instructed.

"The engineer who was being transported from Constantinople... His ship and escort were attacked off the Dalmatian coast. P-Pirates on our side of the blockade. One of the survivors said they were coming from Venice and were flying your personal flag. They thought you had sent a ship to greet them," the man said.

Nico went wholly still in the way only a shifter could. His eyes glowed aqua blue, showing his beast was far too close to the surface. He turned his attention to Gio.

"Now, will you let me deal with the fucking pirate problem?" he demanded.

"You watch that tone when you speak to me, boy," Gio replied so calmly that the hair on the back of Zahir's neck rose. "But, yes, you will be dealing with this pirate problem once and for all. Zahir, Arkon? You will accompany Nico downstairs to speak with the mage. This disguised ship could have been how the little rat got into the city to begin with. Well? Go."

The three of them left without further argument. Arkon and Nico were so worked up, they were positively vibrating.

"You two need to calm down before I take you into the dungeons," Zahir said as they walked. "No one wants to take this man apart more than I do, but you won't get the information you need if you break his jaw."

"Oh, I'll get the information," Nico growled under his breath.

"And how is the lovely Ezra? Have you told her that she is your consort yet?" Arkon asked him.

"Ezra is perfect, and yes, I have."

"A consort?" Nico looked sideways at him. "Do you mean like a mate?"

"Indeed, my serpentine friend," Arkon answered before Zahir could. "Our dear king is all but shacked up with his mage. Which means I'm making you my new drinking buddy. Us smart and single males must stick together."

"For the good of the patriarchy?" Zahir asked with a roll of his eyes.

"Don't be droll. I meant purely for our own entertainment. Not everything in life has to revolve around the fairer sex."

"Says the man most obsessed out of all of us," Zahir said.

"Thank you for the offer, Arkon, but I have pirates to hunt and hang from my mast," Nico replied with a small smile that said he was imagining doing just that.

"Well, we all have our kinks, I suppose," Arkon lamented and opened the door leading into the dungeons from the council chambers.

The dungeons were cool, dank, and an excellent place for despair to grow like mold in the shadows. The Varangian mage was sitting in a cell, apart from the other Cabal members.

Arkon unlocked the mage's cell. He was sleeping peacefully, so Nico grabbed him off the floor by his neck and dropped him onto the only chair in the cell. A med-mage had mended his arm and leg, purely to give Arkon a blank canvas to work with. Vladek looked at Nico with a bored expression. The commander had taken off his blue and silver jacket and was rolling up his long white sleeves.

"Who are you supposed to be?" Vladek asked.

Nico hit him, a perfect fast strike that sent his head backward. "Commander D'Argento. A pleasure to meet you."

Vladek chuckled and spat out a mouthful of blood. "Ah, the *Commander*. I know someone who is your biggest fan."

"And who would that be?" Nico asked, crossing his arms. He was huge and impressive, and if Zahir was being honest, if Nico ever looked at him with that glare, he would've told him whatever he wanted to know.

"Why, the Pirate King, of course."

Arkon and Zahir shook their heads. "Whoops. You just made your last dumb mistake," Arkon said. Nico had the mage pressed against the wall in a move so fast that Zahir didn't follow it. He held the mage with one hand around his throat and high enough that Vladek's feet were dangling off the ground.

"You had better start talking, Varangian, or Nico is going to break every bone in your body," Zahir advised.

"Do that...and you won't ever learn where the Wolf Mage is," Vladek gasped out.

"Oh, yes, we definitely will." Arkon laughed and nodded to Nico. "Have fun. We will be back in twenty minutes."

Nico's eyes glowed. "I won't need twenty minutes."

Arkon locked the door behind them. "Come along, Zahir. We have other people to mess with."

"I had wondered what you did with all the Cabal members. Any of them singing for you yet?" Zahir asked. He had ideas on exactly what he wanted to do with them.

"I put them all together to see who would blame whom. We've only had them turn on one man and beat him to death so far, to silence him, I believe, but I think with a bit more time, we will get what we need," Arkon said cheerily, stopping in front of the door. He pulled back the eye slot.

Zahir's rage simmered hot as he looked at the men all sitting in different parts of the cell. The Cabal hadn't discriminated; there were members from every district in Venice. Zachariah still drew breath, which disappointed him. He saw Zahir and spat. Charming.

"These ones think they are all too loyal and stoic to talk. I thought you would have something more fun to use on them than fists," Arkon said and patted him on the shoulder. "Think of it as an early wedding present."

"You always give me the most thoughtful gifts, *habibi*," Zahir replied. He kissed Arkon on the cheek. "I love it, and so will Ezra."

"You're both very welcome. I do adore her already, so you are lucky she found you first instead of me," Arkon said and gave the Cabal members a friendly little wave.

"You all thought that you could threaten to imprison my people without consequences," Zahir called to them. "You should have listened more closely to your bedtime stories about what happens to those stupid enough to try to trap a djinn. Especially me."

Zahir's hot bronze power shot through the slot in the door. The Cabal members shouted in alarm, trying and failing to get away from the magic. It saturated the cell, filling the men with Zahir's spell. Their eyes glossed over, blind with the magic that struck them down. One by one, they started to sob in terror, their hands flailing about in front of them. Others curled in on themselves, rocking and mumbling.

"What did you do?" Arkon asked curiously.

Zahir smiled, every inch the vengeful king of the djinn. "I am letting them feel what it's like to be trapped alone for centuries. They will be ready to talk for you soon enough, sorcerer," he said and shut the slot on their screams.

CHAPTER THIRTY-TWO

*E*zra was checking on the lamb in the oven when Zahir appeared out of thin air and picked her up to kiss her. She forgot all about the lamb and wrapped her arms and legs around him.

"The council meeting went well then?" she said, coming up for air.

"It did. I also got to enact a little revenge on the bastard Cabal. A good day," he replied, kissing the tip of her nose before setting her down on her feet. "What is all this cooking about?"

"I've invited Stella, Dom, and Arkon around for dinner tonight. I wanted to thank them for everything," she said.

Zahir took a strawberry from the fruit bowl. "Arkon is a little preoccupied at the minute. He and Nico are introducing Vladek to the fine art of Venetian negotiation."

"Do you think Nico will be hungry once they are done? I'll send him an invitation too," Ezra said with an innocent smile.

Zahir's eyes narrowed. "Alas, our handsome Nico is going to be too busy hunting pirates to come and eat. Never get between a male shifter and a hunt."

"Is it like getting between a djinn and over decorating?" Ezra asked cheekily.

Zahir sent a tiny ball of magic to zap her. "You were the one who refused to move."

It was an argument they had more than once over the past week. Ezra had wanted to keep living in her house in the Ghetto Nuovo, and when Zahir had suggested a renovation to make room for him, she had foolishly agreed. She had asked him to leave Judah's study and the library alone. The rest of the house needed a facelift.

Now there was absolutely no mistaking that a djinn lived there. Apart from those rooms, everything else had changed into something that resembled a Moroccan palace. The top floor was now one large bedroom and bathroom with a skylight of brightly colored glass and a small twisting ladder leading up into the now verdant, tropical rooftop garden.

The second floor had become Zahir's study that seemed to have djinn lingering about in it during the daylight hours. Ezra still wasn't sure where the door was leading to it from the outside.

The bottom floor with the study and library was the only thing she recognized. Even the kitchen was different.

"Are you saying you don't like my style, consort?" Zahir asked, nipping at her bottom lip.

"I love it. Otherwise, I would let my magic destroy it and make you do it again," she replied, kissing him back. Ezra was still a little in awe every time he called her consort. What was worse was all the other djinn had started calling her that as well.

"Speaking of your magic, Ashirah has agreed to start teaching you the depth of it and how to wield it," Zahir replied, tucking one of her curls behind her ear.

Ezra lifted a brow. "Really? How did you get her to agree to do that?"

"Easily. I said if she didn't do it, we were going to go and stay with Karsudan so he could teach you. She would be left in charge of Venice while we were gone," Zahir replied with a devious smile. "She readily agreed."

Ezra laughed softly. "Are you sure you don't want to teach me? Ashirah is scary."

"I am a terrible teacher, and I wouldn't be able to keep my hands off you every time you drew on some of my magic," Zahir replied. "We will have to go and see Karsudan soon, though."

"We do? Why is that?" Ezra asked.

Zahir pulled her close, and she slipped her arms around his neck. "Because, my consort, he is going to do the binding ceremony so I can make you mine forever."

"It's barely been a week. You said you would give me time," Ezra replied.

"A week is time," Zahir argued. He turned his head to kiss the golden ring on her index finger. "It was time enough for you to figure out how to unbind me from that ring."

That was true. She had kept the ring on after its power had been broken, wanting a reminder to never lose her path the way her father had.

"I love you, but a week is not enough time," Ezra said and kissed him. She would make him wait at least a month. She wanted to belong to him every way she could. It was the principal of the matter that held her back.

"All right, enough of that, you two," Stella said, coming into the kitchen with black gift bags.

"You're early," Zahir grumbled, letting Ezra go.

"I was bored at home, and Gio has held Dom up for something," Stella replied. She held out one of the bags to him. "A gift from Antonio. He has a new baklava recipe he's been perfecting and wants to know your thoughts."

"Antonio is a saint of a man," Zahir said, taking the bag with a wide smile.

Stella held out the other bag to Ezra. "This is for you. A present from Arkon and I."

"Thank you," Ezra said. Her heart squeezed as she opened the bag. Inside, wrapped in soft velvet, was an urn of black metal. "Is this…"

"It's him. Arkon found out where they had dumped his body in an old grave on San Michele. It wasn't the only one in there either," Stella said softly. "Arkon wanted to make sure he was returned home."

Tears filled Ezra's eyes as she put her arms around Stella. "Thank you so much."

"You're welcome," Stella replied before letting her go.

Zahir's arms came around her instantly, drawing her into his warmth and love. "When you're ready, we can have a ceremony and put him to rest," he said and kissed the few tears that had fallen on her cheeks.

Ezra nodded and kissed him. "I love you."

"I love you too, my sparrow," he replied, his power brushing against hers, so she felt the truth of his words in every part of her.

Ezra took the urn into Judah's study and placed it on the desk next to their family photo. She kissed the top of the cool metal, her heart finally at peace and full of love for the man she had lost and the one she had gained.

"Welcome home, Papa."

FATE AND KINGS

*J*t is time to leave our King of Wands safe in the arms of his lover and sail across the dark Adriatic, where a boat lies, waiting for the gallant Commander D'Argento.

The red glow of a cigarette cherry burns bright, illuminating the emerald green eyes of the Pirate King. Taking a pile of soft, ancient tarot cards, the king shuffles the deck thoughtfully.

They received word that their cargo was spending time in the cells of the Doge's palace and they fled Venice on the high tide.

The king believed that everything happened for a reason, something that was proven when they intercepted a ship carrying an even greater prize than an ill-tempered Varangian mage.

It won't be long now before the Serpent Commander sails straight to them. At last, they will end their battle of cat and mouse.

The king asks Fate for her favor, turns a card, and places it on the deck of the ship. The card shows a faded and forlorn man sitting in a prison of eight swords.

The commander will be in their net in no time.

The Pirate King throws back her head of shining red hair and laughs loudly at the full moon.

And Fate, who always plays fair, laughs back at the Pirate King.

She has no idea what is coming for her.

ABOUT THE AUTHOR

I am a Finnish-Australian writer that is obsessed with magical wardrobes, doors, auroras and burial mounds that might offer me a way into another realm. Until then, I will write about fairy tales, monsters, magic and mythology because that's the next best thing.

Want to say hi? You can find me on Instagram, or get all the latest news by subscribing to my blog newsletter at:
https://amykuivalainenauthor.com/blog-2/

Thank you so much for reading **King of Wands!** If you enjoyed it, please consider leaving a short review or a rating on Amazon, as it helps other readers find my books and means the world to me.

If you are eager for another story filled with fantasy, romance, myth and legend, please keep reading for a sample of 'Wolf of the Sands.'

WOLF OF THE SANDS

1.

Fenrys Rune-Tongue opened her mouth to the sky and let the rainwater drip slowly down her parched throat.

It had been four days since she had been tied to her corner of the longboat. She had lived off the little rainwater she could manage to get into her mouth or suck off the wooden railing she was tied to. Her captors didn't care if she died; they were hoping she would save them the headache of handling her.

In the dark of midnight, the raiders had beached their boat in the bay at her village of Visby, the place of sacrifices, where women came to learn to be seiðr to serve the gods. No one had ever dared attack them. Not until Egil had managed to convince his men it would be easy picking.

Fen had made it harder for them than they expected. She had been trained as a shield maiden and a seiðr, and she had killed seven of the raiders before they managed to overpower her.

It had been sufficient time for the acolytes and the teachers to get away and hide in the forest, and that was enough for Fen.

"We should push her over the side and be done with it," Brandr spat as he glared at her.

Fen smirked. She liked that he was scared of her.

Good.

She was a seiðr, a keeper of stories and magic, a seer and sacred servant of Freya and Odin. Their mistreatment of her was enough for even the strongest of the raiders to be nervous. Egil only laughed at him.

"Don't be a coward. She can do nothing to us without an ax in her hand."

"The seiðr have magic. Who knows what curse she will bring down on us," Brandr argued, earning Egil's fist in his face.

"Shut up. We will be in Hedeby tomorrow, and we will sell her like all the rest."

Fen laughed. "You think anyone is going to buy a seiðr? They will be too scared of the All-Father's wrath as you should be," she said calmly. Brandr raised his fist to her, but Egil caught his arm.

"Leave it. Don't let the witch provoke you," he said. "We are going to sell her to someone who doesn't care about the gods or what powers she might have."

Fen ignored them, settling deeper into her damp blue cloak that still smelled of pine smoke and blood. She tried not to listen as the other female slaves were assaulted that night, as they had been every night since their capture.

She prayed softly to Freya that they would be strong and those who touched them would die screaming and without glory. If she had a chance to get free, she would give them that death for everything they had done.

The goddess's warm presence caressed her, and Fen whispered her gratitude. She was Odin-marked, after all, so the goddess rarely acknowledged her, but Freya was the mother of all seiðr; maybe she would not forget her daughter like Odin had. Fen had saved as many of her priestesses as she could. Perhaps that made Freya look favorably on her.

Fen wanted to know what the fuck the All-Father was

playing at, letting an ox-like Egil take her as a slave. She should have seen their attack in the runes, should have been able to read this journey in her wyrd.

No one had seen it, and that was bad for all of the seiðr.

* * *

The following day, Fen woke to the smell of smoke and a fog so thick, she could barely see the front of the boat. She did her best to wipe the frost off her braid, still stained with blood and mud despite the rain that had been falling on her for days.

As the sun warmed, the fog began to vanish, and the trading port of Hedeby rose out of it—an island of moored boats, raiders, farmers, whores, and foreigners.

"Finally, we can be done with you," Brandr snarled as he directed one of the men to untie her. He wasn't about to lay a hand on her despite his words.

With cramps racing up and down her legs and back, Fen climbed from the boat and onto the wooden jetty to stand with the other twenty slaves. They all looked ashen and not worth the coin Egil would charge for them.

"Walk," Egil commanded, shoving at Fen with the butt of his spear. He wasn't brave or stupid enough to get too close, either. One wrong move, and Fen would have that spear so deep in his gullet that it came out of his throat.

The slaves were herded along the stinking streets, through the fish markets, and where farmers were selling crops. The ring of a blacksmith's forge sounded in the distance, and people were busy selling or buying everywhere. There were also traders from the east—men in richly colored robes selling spices, dyes, and fabrics.

The stench of human suffering, blood, and shit filled Fen's nose as they made it to the slave markets. Women and children were chained in pens, separate from the men, and ranked only slightly higher than livestock.

Fen ground her teeth together at the curse biting at her tongue. She made to follow the women into a pen, but a round shield shoved her back.

"Not you, witch. We would never sell you to this crowd," Brandr said, sharing a smile with Egil. He took the rope of her leash and tugged her along.

There were only the two of them. She would only need a slight distraction. Fen froze as the cold, sharp tip of a spear rested on the back of her neck.

"Don't even think about it. You already cost me seven *vikingar,* and if you weren't worth the gold I need, I would gut you right here," Egil snarled softly. "Now, move."

Fen kept walking, following Brandr and trying to stay out of the way of the crowd. They headed out of town and up a grassy hill.

She wondered if she was being taken to be sacrificed, but no one would pay raiders gold for that, and no one would dare to sacrifice a seiðr.

Cages had been built at the top of the hill, but of metal, not wood. They were filled with criminals and those too dangerous to sell at a regular slave market.

Those hard-faced men all looked like they were going to piss themselves. The slave traders didn't look much happier.

Blank-faced women of all ages were crowded into another cage. Fen couldn't help but notice they were holding up better than the men.

What in Hel's name is going on here?

The caw of a raven made Fen's head snap to the side, and her stomach filled with ice. She hadn't been afraid before, but she was now.

Two stone obelisks rose out of the earth like teeth, strange runes carved into them. They were at least ten feet tall, and sitting on top of each one was a raven watching her.

A Sky Bridge.

She had never seen them but heard the stories and knew to fear them.

All-Father, what did I do to displease you? Fen begged. Surely not something terrible enough to deserve this. She had saved the other seiðr. She had always served the gods loyally. Despite her heartbreak, she would show no fear.

"Good, we made it before they got here," Egil said with a laugh at Fen.

"They are watching us," Brandr whispered, noticing the birds.

"Shut the fuck up. This will be done with soon," Egil replied. "Their gold spends as easily as any other's. The bridge only opens once a year, so any curse for taking the witch will leave when she does."

A pale light began to glow between the pillars, growing brighter as it filled the space. A bronze metal head shaped like a monstrous cat appeared through the light, followed by the rest of an armored body. Four others appeared, all bigger than ordinary men, carrying wickedly curved sickle swords at their sides and shields almost as tall as Fen was.

"You will sell me to the People of Sand and Sky? Do you really not fear the gods, Egil?" Fen demanded, a last pathetic attempt to save herself.

Egil only laughed. "Bitch, the gods won't hear you once you go through the Sky Bridge. Not even Odin himself will be able to see you or hear your prayers."

Fen straightened to her full six feet of height, making the two shorter men step backward in fear of the giantess.

"I pray to Odin that you both live long lives, and you die old men, alone by a hearth and with no honor," she cursed. "You will not see the halls of Valhalla. You will freeze in the wastes of Hel's halls, and no one will remember your name."

Brandr hit her, fear making his face white. Fen tasted iron as she smiled at him and spat on the ground, sealing her curse with blood.

"It doesn't mean shit," Egil said, joining the other traders and the strangely armored men.

"Take it back," Brandr hissed.

"Never," Fen replied, her red-stained smile widening further. Egil whistled at them, and Brandr dragged her forward and thrust her rope at the bronze soldier.

The eyes of the helm were completely black, but Fen could feel them assessing her. A gloved hand touched her long, golden braid, and the warrior nodded. Gold ingots changed hands, and Fen's rope was tied to the train of the other slaves.

The ravens hadn't moved from the top of the glowing Sky Bridge, black eyes watching every moment.

"Why?" she whispered, but no reply came to her. There was no warmth of magic in her fingers or the iron and honey taste of runes on her tongue.

The train of slaves began to move through onto the bridge. As Fen's feet stepped into the burning light, the last thing she knew of Midgard was the black eyes of the ravens and the cold certainty that Odin had abandoned her.

2.

Fen stumbled in surprise as she went through the tunnel of light and into the strangest barn she had ever seen. It was made entirely of a gray-blue metal, with metal grating under her feet and small metal pens that each slave was being directed into.

One of the cat-helmed guards gestured to her, and she stepped inside the nearest one. Before she sensed him move, he locked a metal collar around her throat.

The guard said something to her, but seeing her blank expression, he reached out and fiddled with the band of metal.

"Can you understand me now, slave?" the guard demanded, and Fen nodded.

"Good. It means your collar is doing its job and translating. Take off everything you are wearing and place it on the grid in the back. Don't step on it, or you'll regret it," the guard instructed.

Fen didn't hesitate. The gods hadn't saved her. She didn't expect them to do it now. She unclipped her blue seiðr cloak and pulled off her sodden boots, tunic, and trousers. The guard gestured at the leather ties in her hair, so she unraveled her filthy braid and placed them on her boots. The only item she hesitated over was the Thor's hammer amulet hanging around her neck.

"He's not listening to your prayers either," she said miserably and dropped the necklace on the grid.

As soon as she was naked and shivering, a blue flame leaped up through the holes in the grid, burning all that remained of her past. Fen didn't have time to mourn her possessions. She yelped in surprise as warm water shot out of the small holes in the walls, hosing down all the mud and blood from her hair and body.

What magic are they using to make this happen? Fen couldn't imagine.

There were so few stories of the Sand and Sky people, and those that went through a Sky Bridge never returned to tell anyone what they had seen.

The water stopped only to be replaced by a floral-smelling air jet that dried her off. The guard tossed her a tied bundle, and Fen dressed in an undyed linen dress that came to her knees and tied around her waist. She pulled on the leather sandals as the door to the pen opened. The guard thrust a small amphora at her.

"Drink this and don't spit it out, or I'll have you whipped."

It was sticky and thick, like drinking a herbal tree sap. She gagged twice, but Fen managed to finish it. Her stomach turned as the potion hit it. She doubted they would take her this far to poison her. A dead slave wasn't any use to them.

Not that it mattered anymore. If Odin had really abandoned her, there would be no place in Valhalla for her anymore.

"This one is de-contaminated and ready to be taken out," the guard called, and Fen was hustled back into another line of clean slaves.

"Where do you think they are taking us now?" a small man whispered beside her.

"Probably to work until we die," someone muttered in reply. "A slave life is never one of value. I doubt these people are much better than the fuckers that sold us."

Fen touched the collar at her throat, feeling an engraving stamped into the metal. She looked sideways at the shivering slave beside her and saw that the engraving was of the same type of big cat as the guard's helms. A mark of ownership.

You're lucky. They could be branding your ass like cattle right now.

The slave next to her started sobbing, and Fen stepped away from them, straightening her shoulders. She was a shield maiden; she wasn't going to snivel over the fate the gods had tossed her into, even if she didn't understand it, and she felt alone for the first time in her life.

"Get ready to move out," one of the guards called to the assembled slaves. The blades of their spears lit up with crackling orange light, and several slaves gasped in horror.

"Look at these dumb barbarians! They panic like animals as soon as they see something sparkle," said the guard closest to Fenrys. She fought the urge to take his magic spear and show him just what a dumb barbarian could do with it.

What would be the point? You don't know how to get the Sky Bridge opened anyway.

Fen didn't have time to contemplate it. A roar of metal scraping against metal filled the air as the front of the barn opened to the dazzling sun outside. She had thought the barn was impressive, but nothing could have prepared her for the city outside of it.

They walked out onto a long pier, the broad river full of boats on one side and a city of stone on the other. Fen tilted her head back to stare at the imposing walls and the guards patrolling them.

"Any of you try and run, and you will be executed," the guard leading the column shouted back. Not one of the slaves looked like they would dare.

They crossed through the wooden city gates, following the lead of their guards. The streets were paved in stone, and the houses on either side were two-storied square blocks with mud walls and roofs thatched with reeds.

Brown and black people dressed in colorful robes and loose dresses stared and pointed them out to inquisitive children. One of the bolder boys asked a guard if they were ghosts or monsters. The guard laughed loudly.

"No, child. They are Amun's half-made. That's why they are so small and ugly," he told him.

Fen had never heard of Amun, but she stored the name and information away at the back of her mind, out of habit and training.

On the streets beside them, people rode horses or lumbering animals the color of sand with strange humps. Others were carried in boxes by strong men with slave collars or rode in sleek carriages.

The streets and buildings slowly began to change, becoming cleaner with people dressed more finely. The buildings changed from mud brick to stone. Gardens and trees lined the white stone streets instead of market stalls.

Even the air was different—hot, dry, and smelling of flowers and spices Fen couldn't name. She spotted a shining palace overlooking the city as they passed through a city square.

"Stop gaping and get moving," a guard snapped at her, and Fen put her head down and hurried to catch up with the others.

They entered a new district, and the cat-headed symbols seemed to be stamped into every building and on every flag. They passed pleasure houses with scantily clad men and women gesturing at the guards to come in.

Finally, they turned a steep corner, and Fen gasped. Before

2.

them was one of the biggest buildings she had ever seen. It was built of white stone, with blue columns and flags flying in the breeze. It had three levels, but most confusing of all, it had no roof.

What in Freya's name is this?

"We are all going to die," a man's gruff voice said from behind her.

"Why? What is it?" Fen asked. "Is it a temple?"

"No. That's an arena, woman. We are going to die bloody."

"Silence!" a guard shouted at them.

A tall wooden gate swung open, and they were led through training areas, with big men shooting arrows and throwing spears at dummies. Some were sparring and teasing each other. Some stopped and looked at the groups of slaves with open disgust.

The guards made them stop in front of a balcony overlooking the training yards. A tall man with a shaved head and dressed in shimmering blue robes looked down at them with critical eyes. Fen forced herself to stare back at him.

"I am Nektos of the House of Sekhmet, and you are now my property," he called down to them. "Serve me well, and you will find I am a gracious master. Disobey me, and you will die screaming. That is all." He waved a long hand at the guards to move them on. He leaned over to a woman with a board and said some words to her before disappearing from sight.

"Get moving!" the guard commanded, and they started walking again.

A high-pitched screech shook the training grounds, and pure terror streaked through Fen's veins. The slaves cried out, making the guards laugh.

"Ignorant barbarians," one guard complained.

They were herded around the corner of the building, and Fen's mouth fell open in awe. Massive creatures were being

201

transported in cages and were unlike anything Fen had ever seen. They had wings, disfigured bird heads, and cat bodies.

"That's your fate if you don't prove yourself worthy. The chimeras love to eat disobedient slaves," the guard nearest her said and pushed her forward.

"Don't lie to them," another guard chided. "They will all be chimera food before the week is out."

Fen swallowed down her fear. She had seen falcons and ravens tear through their prey and the dead. She could only wonder what these creatures would do.

The woman she had seen with Nektos met the guards by an archway. The guards all bowed like she was someone important. She was beautifully dressed in the same blue as all the flags.

"Nektos wants the best and strongest to attend the Feast of Sacrifices tonight," she said primly. She looked Fen over. "This one too. He thinks the bidding on her will be good because of her unique coloring, and the men that sold her claimed she was a warrior."

"She looks too scrawny to be a warrior, Azra," the guard said, looking Fen over.

"Then she'll die in sacrifice to Sekhmet. Make sure they are all cleaned up and ready by sundown."

Fen's hands clenched at her sides, and she prayed to Freya. The goddess's rune mark on her thumb burned, and Fen managed a small smile. Freya hadn't abandoned her, not even in this place.

Freya was the goddess of war as well as magic, and Fen had battle songs in her veins. She had been blessed by the other war god, Týr, before being given to the seiðr. She knew his victory runes and how to call on him for aid. She would not be broken by the collar around her neck or the manacles on her arms.

If she died and Odin refused to welcome her to Valhalla, she would walk into the frozen halls of Niflheim with her head high.

If her blood was going to be used as a sacrifice, it sure as Hel wouldn't be in honor of Sekhmet. She would make sure of it.

* * *

Need more Fen? 'Wolf of the Sands' is available now from all book retailers!

ALSO BY AMY KUIVALAINEN

THE MAGICIANS OF VENICE

The Immortal City

The Sea of the Dead

The King's Seal

THE FIREBIRD FAERIETALES

Cry of the Firebird

Ashes of the Firebird

Rise of the Firebird

THE TAROT KINGS

King of Swords

King of Wands

STANDALONE

Sorcerers and Saints

Wolf of the Sands